Praise for Anne Tyler

"One of the most beguiling and mesmerizing writers in America."

"Not me

"A novel
A very fu
ful writer

"Tyler's
angles of
monic lor

"Her peop

ALSO BY ANNE TYLER

A
SLIPPING-DOWN
LIFE

Anne Tyler

Fawcett Columbine • New York

A Fawcett Columbine Book
Published by Ballantine Books

A somewhat abridged form of this novel appeared in the January
1970 issue of *Redbook* magazine.

http://www.randomhouse.com

Library of Congress Catalog Card Number: 97-90337

ISBN: 0-449-00102-4

This edition published by arrangement with Alfred A. Knopf, Inc.

Manufactured in the United States of America

First Ballantine Books Mass Market Edition:October 1992
First Ballantine Books Trade Edition: July 1997

10 9 8 7 6 5 4 3 2 1

1

E vie Decker was not musical. You could tell that just
   from the way she looked—short and wide, heavy-
footed. She listened to marches without beating time,
forgot the tune to "The Star-Spangled Banner," and
moved soddenly around the high school gym in a bum-
bling two-step. At noon, while Evie munched a sand-
wich, boys from the band played Dixieland in a corner
of the cafeteria. Sharp brass notes pierced the air above
the tables; they darted past like red and yellow arrows.
Evie ate on, a plump drab girl in a brown sweater that
was running to balls at the elbows.

So when she invited Violet Hayes (her only friend)
to a rock show at the Stardust Movie Theater, Violet
couldn't understand it. "What would you go to a thing
like that for?" she said. "Are you serious? I don't believe you even know what a rock show is."

"Well, I do listen to the radio," Evie said.

And she did. She listened all the time. With no company but her father and the cleaning girl (and both of
them busy doing other things, not really company at
all) she had whole hours of silence to fill. She turned
her radio on in the early morning and let it run while
she stumbled into her clothes and unsnarled her hair.
In the afternoons, advertisements for liver pills and
fertilizers wove themselves in among her homework as-

1

signments. She fell asleep to a program called "Sweet-heart Time," on which a disc jockey named Herbert read off a list of names in twos to dedicate each song. "For Buddy and Jane, for Sally and Carl, for George and Sandra, he loves her very much. . . ." Herbert was an old man with a splintery voice, the only disc jockey the station had. He read the dedications haltingly, as if they puzzled him. "For Paula and Sam, he hopes she'll forgive last night . . ." and there would be the rustle of a paper lowered and a pause for him to stare at it. At the end of a song he said, "That was the Rowing—the Rolling Stones." His faltering made him sound sad and bewildered, but no more bewildered than Evie.

She listened carefully. She lay on her back in the dark, wearing a great long seersucker nightgown, and frowned at the chinks of light that shone through the radio's seams. Sometimes the names were familiar to her—couples she had watched floating hand in hand down school corridors in matching shirts, or girls called Zelda-Nell or Shallamoor, so that they couldn't hope to pass unnoticed. When she knew the names she paid close attention to the songs that followed, ferreting out the words with a kind of possessiveness but ignoring the tunes. Pop songs and hard rock and soul music tumbled out of the cracked brown portable, but the only difference she heard between them was that the words of the pop songs were easier to understand.

One evening in February there was a guest on the program. He came right after the "News of the Hour." "I have here a Mr. Bertram Casey," said Herbert. "Better known as, known as Drumstrings." He coughed and shuffled some papers. "It's an honor to have you with us, Mr. Drumstrings."

No one answered.

Evie was sitting on the bed, twisting her hair into scratchy little pincurls. When the silence grew noticeable she took a bobby pin from her mouth and looked at the radio. All she heard was static. Finally Herbert said, "Well. This is the beginning of a new feature on 'Sweetheart Time': interviews. May I ask if you are a native North Carolinian, Mr. Drumstrings?"

Someone said, "Not for long I won't be."

His voice was cool and motionless, like a stone plunked into a pool. Herbert coughed again.

"*Whereabouts* in North Carolina?" he asked.

"Farinia."

"Farinia, yes. Off of Highway—"

"But I'm leaving there," said Drumstrings Casey.

"All right. Where is it you're going?"

"A city, some city. It ain't quite clear yet. I aim to cut records and play night clubs, and if I once wiggle out of here I'm never coming back again, not even for Christmas. If my family gets to missing me they can come to where I'm at, I'll buy them a house with white telephones and a swimming pool."

"That's very nice," said Herbert. "Have you done much recording yet?"

"No."

"What are the names of your, um, records?"

"There ain't none."

"Oh. Well, your style, then. Would you care to describe it for us?"

"Style?"

"Your style."

"Style, *ain't* no *style*."

"Well, what, what do you *do*, exactly?"

This pause was even longer than the first one. Second after second ticked away in dead air. "If you don't know what I do," said Drumstrings finally, "then how come you got me on your program?"

Herbert mumbled something.

"What's that?"

"Because they told me to, I said. Heavens, boy, just answer the questions. Let's get this over with."

"Oh," Drumstrings said. "All right."

"Only thing they gave me was a little scrap of paper with your name on it."

"Well, don't blame me. I just show up where I'm asked for."

"All right, all right. Where was I?"

"You want to know what I do. I sing and play guitar. Rock."

"You have one of those groups," Herbert said.

"I sing alone. All I got is a drummer, but I don't know about him."

"How's that?"

"He kind of trods the beat."

"Oh, yes," said Herbert.

There was a series of tiny explosions; someone was tapping his fingers.

"You could ask me where I get my material," Drumstrings said.

"Where do you get your material?"

"I make it up."

"That's very interesting."

"Some is other people's, but most is my own. I make it up in my room. I lie on my bed arguing with the strings, like, and sooner or later *something* comes out. Then my fingers get to hammering, reason they call me Drumstrings. How many people do you know could carry a set of drums singlehanded with one little old electric guitar? Lots will say you can't do it. *I* can. I don't go along with all them others. Well: how my songs start. Words come out. Things I hear. 'Oh, Lord, why can't you ever come home on time like decent people do. . . .' " He was singing now, and his fingers kept a beat upon a hard surface. The suddenness of it surprised Herbert into clearing his throat, but Evie listened without changing expression, chewing absently on the rubber tip of a bobby pin. "Nothing more to it," said Drumstrings. "Just putting hard rhythm to what floats around in parlors, just hauling in words by their tails. Nothing more."

"Is that right," said Herbert.

Drumstrings Casey was silent again.

"Do you think we—well, I guess we covered near about everything now. Folks, say good-bye to—"

"Good-bye," the cool voice said.

"And give him a nice hand."

But there was no one to give him a hand, of course—only the Beatles, starting up brokenly in the middle of a line, hurried-sounding, without any list of names to lead them in.

"Do you know a singer named Drumstrings Casey?" Evie asked the boy behind her in algebra class. He was a bongo player. Sometimes she heard him whistling soundlessly at the back of her neck, tapping out the beat on his desk and moving his shoulders in rhythm. But, "Never heard of him," he said.

"He's a rock-and-roll singer."

"Rock-and-roll is *out* now."

"Oh, I see," said Evie.

She walked most places alone. She carried her books clutched to her chest, rounding her shoulders. Her face, which was pudgy and formless, poked itself too far forward. And like most heavy people, she had long ago stopped expecting anything of her clothes. Her coat was old-fashioned, wide-shouldered, falling in voluminous uneven folds around her calves. The white collar she wore to brighten her complexion had a way of twisting sideways and riding up her neck, exposing a strip of skin above the collar of her coat. When classmates met up with her they passed in a hurry, barely noticing her. Evie never spoke to them. She bent to pull up a swallowed sock, or tied the knotted laces of her oxfords. Then she walked on.

On her way home from school one day, she saw a poster in a laundromat window. "Rock the Nite Away!" it said. "Pulqua's first all-local rock show!" Below that was a column of names that she had never heard of: the Huddlers, Spoony and James, Daphne Liggett. And at the bottom, Drumstrings Casey. "Bertram 'Drumstrings' Casey." The name had a worn, vulnerable look, like something she was too familiar with. She pulled a scrap of paper from a frayed zipper notebook and wrote down the time and place of the show. Then she folded the paper and placed it inside her history book.

"Are you serious?" Violet said on the phone. "I don't believe you even know what a rock show is."

"Well, I do listen to the radio."

"What's that got to do with it? You're sitting in your bedroom, listening to the radio. But do you know what kind of trash goes to a live rock show?"

"I don't care," Evie said. She was shut up in her closet to avoid being heard by Clotelia, the cleaning girl. Her voice was muffled by clothes and boots and suitcases, and what was meant to sound lighthearted came out secretive and urgent. "It's at the movie house.

What could happen there? I think we should go, Violet."

"Well, listen," said Violet. "My uncle went to one of those shows in Raleigh, back before he was married. He said they danced the dirty bop all up and down the aisles. He said he was so embarrassed he just sat transfixed to his seat, never saw anything like it."

"What's the dirty bop?" Evie asked.

"*I* don't know."

"Well, it's bound to be out of style by now. They wouldn't still be doing it."

"No, but they'll have thought of something else," Violet said.

"That's all right. I want to hear just one special singer. Then we can go."

"Really? What's his name?"

"Oh, it's nobody famous."

"What's his *name*?"

"Bertram Drumstrings Casey."

"Drumstrings?"

"Do you know him?" Evie asked.

"No. How do *you* know him?"

"I don't. I just heard him on the radio."

"What kind of stuff does he do?"

"I only heard him talking."

"Well, for heaven's sake," said Violet. But she seemed to be thinking it over, because after a minute she said, "Did you ask your father about it?"

"No," Evie said. Her father was a high school math teacher, a vague, gentle man who assumed that Evie would manage just fine wherever she was. In her talks with Violet, though, he kept turning out to be the kind of father who put his foot down. "I don't think I'll bother him with it," she said.

"Oh-oh."

"Will you come?"

"Oh, well, sure," said Violet. "Now that I know the reason why."

When she had hung up, Evie waited a second and then gave her closet door a sudden shove. But Clotelia was nowhere around. Downstairs a soap-opera star said, "This is going to be very hard for me to tell you, Bertha—"

"Oh, Bertha, watch *out!*" Clotelia shouted.

Evie got to her feet and smoothed her wrinkled skirt down.

Violet met her in the lobby, wearing a purple spring coat. She was an enormously fat girl with teased black hair and a beautiful face, and she always wore brilliant colors as if she hadn't read any advice to the overweight. Beside her, Evie seemed almost thin, but lifeless—gray-skinned and dull-haired. She had on her school coat and oxfords. "Are you going to dance in *those?*" Violet said.

"Who would I dance with?"

They were shoved by slick-haired boys in leather jackets, girls in tight sweaters and false eyelashes the size of small whiskbrooms. Almost nobody from school was there. "We are cut off from civilization here. I hope you realize that," said Violet. "I swear, will you look at that girl's *earrings?*" Her voice was rich and and lazy. Every time she spoke, boys turned to see who she was and then slid their eyes away again.

Inside the theater they had to work their way through more boys who roamed the aisles in packs. Above the "No Smoking" signs, blue smoke was already beginning to haze the ceiling. Couples with their arms around each other leaned against walls and exit doors and the pipe railing down front—anywhere but in the chairs.

"Are we supposed to stand during this?" Evie asked, and Violet said, "No, not me." She flung herself into one of the wooden seats, bought second-hand from a larger town nearby. A boy who was sidling down their row said, "*Move* sweetie."

"Move yourself," Violet said.

Oh, nothing bothered Violet. She smiled a beautiful bland smile at the empty stage, and the boy struggled past her large pale knees and then past Evie's, muttering all the time. "You'd think they would serve popcorn," Violet said calmly. She smoothed her skirt down and went on gazing at the stage.

But the popcorn stand was closed tonight. The theater had turned into something else, like a gym transformed for a senior prom or an American Legion hall into a banquet room. There was a cavernous chill from the tongue-and-groove walls, in spite of the heavy velvet window curtains. The ceiling seemed higher and dingier, and when Evie looked up she saw light-fixtures poised dizzyingly far above her, their bowls darkened by pools of insects that she had never noticed before. Down front the movie screen had been rolled up. The wooden stage with its electric amplifiers looked like a roomful of refrigerators. A man in shirt sleeves was unraveling microphone cords. "Testing," he said. "Anybody out there?" The volume was high, but it melted away among the voices in the audience.

When the first group began, only a few people had found seats. Four boys in pink satin shirts came out carrying instruments and stood in a semicircle, and one of them spent some time getting his French cuffs adjusted. Then they began playing. Their music was too loud to be heard. It blended with the voices out front, the volume reaching a saturation point so that it was impossible to separate the notes or distinguish the words. "This is *hurting*," said Violet, but she had to shout directly into Evie's ear. Nobody else seemed to mind. They shuffled about in groups, not quite dancing, or draped themselves on the arms and backs of the seats and snapped their fingers and wagged their heads as they continued their conversations. When the music stopped, they cheered. After three more numbers they clapped raggedly and the musicians gathered their instruments and left. Nobody watched them go.

"Who was that?" Violet asked. But they had no program to tell them. A few minutes later three boys and a girl came on, and the girl sang a song and did a tiny intricate dance step. The words of the song were slippery and whining: *"Oh, ya, ya, my honey knows how. . . . "* Evie felt a sort of seeping discomfort, but the rest of the audience listened carefully and clapped and whistled afterward.

Following the fourth group, there was an intermission. A phonograph somewhere played a Mantovani record. A few of the boys went out to the Coke machines in the lobby, and others took flat curved bottles from their hip pockets. Only Evie and Violet stayed in their seats. They had kept their coats on, as if they were only dropping in on their way to somewhere else. "Where is Drumstrings Casey?" Violet asked. "Was he one of them?"

"No. I don't think so."

"How will we know him?"

"He will only have a drummer. Look, maybe we should go. Do you want to?"

"What for?"

"I feel like I've made a mistake. Shall we go?"

"Oh, why? I'm enjoying myself," Violet said. "At least let's stay till Drumstrings comes."

Drumstrings Casey was preceded by a blond boy who

set out drums in a circle around a stool. The largest drum had a blurry black "Casey" stamped on it with a grocery store stencil. "Now," Evie said. She sat up straighter, clutching her coat across her chest. A dark boy had followed the blond one out. He had long black hair, too shiny, cut square across his neck and falling in a slanted line over his forehead. His clothes were black denim, a short zippered jacket and tight jeans ending in high leather boots. Instead of walking, he glided. His spangled guitar dragged a tail of cord which the drummer took charge of while Casey slid coolly on, almost keeping time with Mantovani's violin. "Cut it," someone shouted. Mantovani stopped playing in the middle of a note. There was a second of pure silence while the blond boy seated himself at the drums. Then he picked up the sticks. He set up a rapid, choppy rhythm that made the dark boy's foot tap, and after that one second of silence, Drumstrings Casey's guitar-playing seemed to break the air into splinters around Evie's ears.

If there were words to his song, Evie couldn't make them out. She heard a clanging of guitar strings, a patter of drums which sometimes subdued the guitar into a mere jingle at the end of a beat, and a strong reedy voice that softened consonants and spun out vowels. "Nnhnn," he said occasionally, close to the microphone. Then the singing stopped, but the music went on. Drumstrings turned his narrow, unseeing face toward the audience.

"Why do you walk on my nerves this way?" he asked suddenly.

Evie turned and looked around her.

"Have I got to tell you again? Have I got to say it?

"We met him on the mountain. He was picking blueberries.

"She was emptying trashcans.
"Don't leave now!"
The guitar grew louder, and the drums along with it.
The song started up no different than before, with the
same blurred words. Not many people clapped when it
was over.

"Well, thank you for coming," Evie told Violet as they
were starting home.
"Was it like you expected?"
"Oh, more or less."
They crossed a silent, neon-lit street. Watery reflec-
tions of themselves slid along an optician's darkened
window.
"What I meant," said Violet, "was Drumstrings
Casey—was *he* like you expected?"
"Not exactly," Evie said.
"You sorry you went?"
"Well, no."
She paused at the corner, in front of the town library.
Their paths were supposed to split here, but instead of
turning down Hawthorne Street, Evie stood still with
her hands in her pockets and her oxfords set wide apart.
"That speaking out he did," she said.
"That *was* peculiar," said Violet. "I never heard
anyone do that before."
"Me neither."
"Well, in slow songs, of course. Those sappy kinds
of songs, some girls reading out a love letter between
two verses."
"This is different. Drumstrings Casey wasn't sappy."
"No."
"What," said Evie. "You liked it?"
"Well, yes, I did."
"Me too." Evie started moving one foot in a slow

arc in front of her, watching it closely. "It made me want to answer. You know those girls who scream on the Ed Sullivan show? Well, now I know why they do it."

"Of course, he is kind of trashy," said Violet.

"Sure, I know that."

"That greasy hair."

"Those tight pants."

"Walking that slinky way he has."

"Would you like to come to my house for a Coke?" Evie asked.

"Oh, I might as well."

They both turned down Hawthorne Street, ambling in fits and starts toward the yellow light above Evie's porch.

≀≀≀

2

A fter the show the days seemed longer and duller. Evie walked to school at a slow, aimless pace, stopping often to stare into store windows. She had changed to spring clothes by now. Her skirts were full, with waistbands that kept folding in upon themselves, her sleeveless blouses came untucked and her sandal straps slipped off her heels—all problems needing constant attention. She walked along continually tugging at hems and rebuttoning buttons, as if she were nervous. Yet her face, seen close to, was blank and listless. She complained to Violet that she had nothing to look forward to. "Summer is coming," she said, "and there I'll be on the porch. Getting fatter. Reading romances. My father will be home all day just picking at the lawn. Don't you wish there was something to do?"

"You could be a camp counselor," Violet said.

Evie only sighed and yanked at a slip strap.

In the changing-room, on gym days, half-dressed girls sat on long wooden benches and named their favorite singers. Their lockers were lined with full-color pictures of the Beatles and the Monkees, their notebooks were decorated with the titles of the top forty, and they traded stacks of pulpy gray magazines filled with new lyrics and autographed photos. Their favorites lived in Detroit or Nashville or London, and switched like baseball players from one group to another, from group-singing to solo, and from an outdated style to a new one. Evie couldn't keep up with them. While the others talked she dressed behind a slatted partition, shielding the front of her 40-D bra as she reached for a blouse, concentrating glumly on what she overheard.

"Fill in your name, they say. Mail it off. If you win you get a date with the singer of your choice, dinner and dancing and a photograph to remember it by. It tells you right here, see?"

"Yes, but what if I win?"

"Lucky you."

"I mean, wouldn't you *die*?"

"Not me."

"I would. I wouldn't say a word all evening. How could you talk to a singing star?"

"That's why you have to watch who you pick. You can't just choose for looks, you got to get someone with personality."

"Paul McCartney has personality."

"His name isn't on here."

One day a tenant farmer's daughter named Fay-Jean Lindsay said, "Those people in the magazines are all right, I reckon. Those Rolling Stones and all. But me, I'll take Joseph Ballew."

"Never heard of him," someone said.

"He's from Pulqua. Right around Pulqua."

"How come we never heard of him?"

"*I* don't know. You ought to have. He sings real nice."

"Where's he at now?"

"Pulqua."

"Well, for heaven's sake," they said, and then they changed the subject.

But later, when Evie was fully dressed, she came out

from behind her partition to talk to Fay-Jean. Fay-Jean was kneeling on the end of a bench, drawing her comb through a ribbon of pale, shining hair. "I heard you liked Joseph Ballew," Evie said.

Fay-Jean tucked away the comb and brought out a mirror, which she looked into for some time. There was nothing else to do with it. She had one of those tiny, perfect faces, not yet sharpened enough to show the tenant farmer in her. "Who?" she said finally.

"Joseph Ballew."

"He's all right."

"Was he at that rock show a few weeks back?"

Fay-Jean looked up. "Why, yes, he was," she said. "I didn't see *you* there."

"I was near the back."

"Did you like him?"

"Well, really I—which one was he?"

"Oh, you couldn't have overlooked him. He sang 'Honeypot.' Now you remember."

"Well," said Evie. "I was wondering. Do you know Drumstrings Casey?"

"Him? Wait a minute."

Fay-Jean started rummaging through her notebook. She came up with red-slashed quizzes, a *Silver Screen* magazine, and finally a sheet of ruled paper which she handed to Evie. It was a pencil drawing of a narrow-faced boy with high cheekbones, one eye smaller than the other. His features were vague, hairy lines, and his mouth had been erased several times and redrawn heavily. "Who's this?" Evie asked.

"It's Drumstrings Casey, who do you think."

"Do you know him?"

"No. Do you think it's a good likeness?"

"Oh, well, sure," said Evie. "But how were you— did you ask him to sit for it?"

"No, I did it at the Unicorn. That's where he plays, same as Joseph Ballew. Joseph Ballew is my real favorite, but I think this one is kind of cute too. You ever been to the Unicorn?"

"I don't even know what it is," Evie said.

"It's a roadhouse. Just south of Pulqua a ways. You can come with me sometime, I got a car I can borrow."

"Tomorrow?"

"What?"

"Are you going there tomorrow?"

"Tomorrow's Friday. Casey only plays on Saturdays."

"Will you be going there this Saturday?"

"Sure, I guess so."

"I'll come with you then," Evie said. "Could I bring a friend?"

"Sure. And keep the picture, if you like."

"Well, thank you. I don't have anything to trade for it."

"To—?"

"Trade. Trade for the picture."

"Why would you want to trade for it?"

"I don't know," Evie said.

She pasted the picture in the middle of her mirror. Drumstrings Casey's penciled head took the place of her own every time she combed her hair. "When we go to the Unicorn," Violet said, "bring a camera. Hanging out with the likes of Fay-Jean Lindsay is bad enough; I fail to see how you can live with her art work."

"I don't mind," Evie said.

The Unicorn was out in the country, a gray windowless rectangle on a lonesome highway with darkness closing in all around it. Cars and motorcycles and pickup trucks

sat any old way in a sand parking lot. In front, beside
a baggy screen door, stood a policeman with his arms
folded. It was not a place that people dressed up for,
but Evie and Violet didn't know that. They came wearing full, shiny dresses and high-heeled pumps. Fay-Jean
had on a skirt and blouse decorated with poodles on
loops of real chain, and she twirled her car keys light-
heartedly around her index finger as she passed the
policeman.

It seemed to be noise that bellied the screen out—
pieces of shouts and guitars and drums and an angry
singer. Noise hit Evie in the face, on a breath of beer
and musty-smelling wood. Someone wanted pretzels,
not potato chips. Someone wanted to know where
Catherine had gone. The singer's voice roughened and
he sang out:

> *You ask me to be somebody I'm not,*
> *How can you say you're my honeypot?*

"Hear that?" Fay-Jean said.

Evie thought if she heard any more the noise would
turn visible.

She followed Fay-Jean through darkness, past rows
of long tables and seated couples. Once she nearly
tripped over someone's outstretched leg. When they
came to a table that had room for them, she found that
a hand holding a lighted cigarette rested on the back of
her chair. "Excuse me!" she shouted. Her voice disappeared as soon as it left her mouth. Finally Fay-Jean
reached over and lifted the hand away, and Evie pulled
her chair out.

"What did you do with that ring I bought?" the singer
asked. He stood under a dim red bulb, moving constantly in a small circle as he sang. *"You ain't* acting

like no honeypot.'' Besides his guitar there were three
other instruments and possibly a piano, although Evie
couldn't be sure. All she saw was someone soundlessly
pressing the keys. Behind them, on the same platform,
a few people danced. The smell of beer gave the air a
cold feeling. The rough walls and tables, built of the
grayed wood used in picnic pavilions, made the building seem flimsy and temporary.

A fat man in a butcher's apron was handing out beer.
When he started toward them Fay-Jean shouted, "How
old are you?"

"Seventeen," said Evie.

"How old is Violet?"

"I'm eighteen," Violet said. "I caught scarlet fever
in the fourth grade and was held—"

"What?"

"Eighteen, I said."

"You're okay. *You*—" and she pointed to Evie, "go
way over. Say you're twenty. Then they won't ask for
proof."

But the fat man did not even question her. He wanted
to see Fay-Jean's driver's license, which she showed
him. Then he looked over at Evie, slumped against the
table with her arms folded under the billowing bosom
of her dress. "What's for you?" he said.

"What?"

"Budweiser," Fay-Jean told him.

"Same for you, ma'am?"

Violet nodded.

Joseph Ballew left the platform. The dancers remained, pivoting on their heels and gazing around the
room, until someone started a record of Frank Sinatra
singing "Young at Heart." Then they gave up and wandered back to their seats.

"That Joseph Ballew is my ideal," Fay-Jean said.

"You can *have* your big names, I don't care. He is only nineteen but looks twenty-five, at least, those two cool lines running down alongside his mouth."

"Have you ever gone up and talked to him?" Evie asked.

"Oh, sure, all the time. Once I called him on the phone and he let on he was busy, but I could tell he was right tickled to be called."

"What would you *say* if you went up?" Evie asked.

"Why, anything that comes to your head. You'll see. Aren't you going to go talk to Casey?"

"Oh, I couldn't," Evie said.

Her beer was brought to her in a chipped glass mug. She took small sips of it and looked sideways at the other customers.

"Once," said Fay-Jean, "a girl fell out, right about where I am sitting. She was listening to the music and then the next thing you know had fell out. Laying out on the floor with her eyes shut. I would have been right embarrassed, if I was her."

"Who was it over?" Violet asked. "Drumstrings Casey or Joseph Ballew?"

"What? Oh, I don't know. It turned out to be a fit of some kind, nothing either of them bothered taking credit for. I will say this, though, she got a right smart of attention for it. They had to lay her out clear across a table. When she came to, Casey said, 'This here is for that pretty little girl yonder on the table,' and he played her a song. It was all wasted, though. Seems she didn't even know she had fell out; she just slid down to her seat and looked around her for some time, smiling kind of baffled-like."

"Is that right?" Evie said. She studied the foam on her beer a minute. Then she said, "Well, talking about attention. Would it cause a fuss if I were to snap his picture? I brought my Kodak.''

"Oh, I thought I had give you that portrait," Fay-Jean said.

"You did," Violet told her. "I remember it, clearly."

"Well, I can't see how taking a picture would do any harm. Joseph Ballew once had a lady here snapping photos all evening long, writing him up for a motel newspaper."

Drumstrings Casey slid onto the platform as silently and as easily as some dark fish, the spangles on his guitar flashing dapples of red light. Nobody hushed or looked in his direction. He might have been anyone. Yet his face, which was a smooth olive color, gave off a glow across the cheekbones and down the bridge of his nose, and surely the audience must have noticed the separate, motionless circle of air he moved in. He hooked a chair with the toe of his boot and slid it to the center of the platform. With one foot resting on it he stared out over Evie's head, and the blond boy ambled forth from behind an amplifier to seat himself at the drums. "Where is the drum with 'Casey' on it?" Evie asked Violet.

"How should I know?"

"He should be using his own drums."

"Maybe these are better."

"I wish he'd use his own. These could be just anyone's."

"Maybe it's too hard to set them up each time. What difference does it make?"

"Well, still," Evie said.

They played a song called "My Girl Left Home." All Evie understood were the first four words. Halfway through, the music slowed and Drumstrings frowned.

"Hold on," he said.

The audience stopped talking.

"She left, you say?"
He hit one note several times over.
"Where were you? Did you see her go?
"The meter man's coming.
"Buy the tickets. Wait in the lobby.
"Have you noticed all the prices going up?"
"My girl left home!" the drummer called. As if that had reminded him, Casey hit all the strings at once and continued with his song. Here and there conversation picked up again, but a few girls stayed quiet and kept their eyes on the guitar strings.

Fay-Jean danced with a boy chewing bubble gum. At the end of the first song she rested her hand on his shoulder and talked about something, steadily. Then a new piece began and another boy took the first one's place. She talked to him too, looking out toward the audience as if what she said took no thought. Her feet wove a curved, slithering pattern on the bare floorboards. The music seemed familiar. It was probably the song Drumstrings Casey had played at the rock show; but then when he slowed his guitar and spoke out, where was the man picking berries and the woman emptying trashcans? This time, he told about someone throwing soda-bottle caps at the moon. And then a bicycle.

"Basket on the front. Shiny in the dark.
"If I tell you again, will you listen this time?
"Never mind."
The song went on. Evie fumbled in her handbag for her camera, and then without allowing herself to think ahead she stood up and aimed it at the platform. Casey looked out beyond her. "Casey!" she called. He turned, still playing, not seeing. When the flashbulb went off he blinked and his eyes snagged on her. "Oho, she lied," he sang, and studied her white, shaky face. Then she sat down. He looked out beyond her again. Her

hands were so tight upon the camera that the circulation seemed to have stopped.

"Evie, I declare," Violet said.

Evie said nothing.

He sang someone else's song next, one she had heard before on "Sweetheart Time." When his guitar slowed, the drummer beat louder, prodding him to hurry, and Drumstrings didn't speak out after all. At the end he bent his head slightly. It must have been a bow; everyone clapped.

After that he walked off the platform and past Evie's table. An envelope of cold air traveled with him, as if he had just come in from a winter night. Evie heard his denim jacket brush Violet's chair, and when she felt that it was safe she turned to look after him. But he had not passed by, after all. He stood behind her with his chin tilted up, his eyes on her beneath half-shut lids.

"You from some newspaper?" he asked.

"No," said Evie.

"Oh," he said, and then he walked on out.

" 'Oh,' he said. Was it 'oh'? Or 'Well.' I should have had an answer planned."

"It's not something you would have expected, after all," Violet said. She was spending the night with Evie, up in her flowered bedroom where the radio still spun music out. They were the only ones awake in the house. They had come home late, packed three abreast in the front seat of Fay-Jean's father's Studebaker, while a bushel basket full of tools rattled around in the back. Now Violet sat yawning and blinking as she unpinned her hair, but Evie was wide awake. She wandered around the room fully dressed, snapping pictures. "I want to use up the film," she said.

"Wait till tomorrow, why don't you?"

"I want to drop it off at the drugstore tomorrow. Is Lowry's open on Sunday? Do you think that his picture will turn out halfway decent?"

"Oh, I imagine so." Violet yawned again and reached for her comb.

"Once I was standing up, I couldn't think what to call him," Evie said. "Bertram or Drumstrings." She photographed her bulletin board, hung with programs and newspaper clippings and a hall pass handwritten by a man teacher whom she had liked the year before. Then she said, "It's those quotes that confuse me. 'Drumstrings' in quotation marks. Which does that mean I should call him by?"

"Like Nat 'King' Cole."

"Oh, that's right. I'd forgotten. What did they call him?"

"Nat."

"Then I should have called him 'Bertram.' But I could never do that. I'd feel silly saying 'Bertram.' " She snapped her own picture in the full-length mirror. "I was so scared, I was shaking," she said.

"I know. I saw."

"My hands were shaking. You mean it showed?"

"Well, I was right next to you."

"It wasn't something I had thought up first, you know. It was spur-of-the-moment. 'Why not?' I thought, and did it. Just stood up and did it." She turned toward Violet, who had lain down on the other side of the bed. "*Impulse.* That's what it was."

"Right," Violet said with her eyes closed.

"If I'd thought before, I would have fallen on my face. Or dropped the camera. Or lost my voice. Impulse was the clue. Are you listening?"

There was no answer. Evie fitted another flashbulb into her camera and snapped Violet's sleeping face.

3

Fay-Jean Lindsay was always dancing, and sometimes going off to huddle in dark cars with boys who
only showed up once. She wasn't the kind to chauffeur
two girls around indefinitely. So Evie and Violet started
borrowing their fathers' cars, taking turns at it, and
coming to the Unicorn by themselves every Saturday
night. They still sat at Fay-Jean's table, although gen-
erally her chair was empty and her purse left spilled
open beside her beer mug. They wore skirts and blouses
now, and waved when they passed the policeman at the
door. Evie's skirts were dark, to slim her down. Her
blouses were white cotton that turned gray and limp
halfway through the evening. Violet's skirts were rose
and purple and chartreuse. She seemed to have taken
the place over for her own—striding between chairs like
a huge, stately queen, serene in the face of whistles and
catcalls, ordering draft beer by the pitcher and pouring
it expertly down the side of her mug so that there would
be no foam. She reminded Evie of the lady chaperones
she had learned about in Spanish class, except that Violet did no chaperoning: Fay-Jean returned from long
absences with unknown partners, tilting against their
shoulders like a solemn rag doll, and Drumstrings Casey
slid his hips in easy circles under Violet's calm gaze.
She said she liked this kind of life. "I should be a

barmaid,'' she said. When a boy at the next table said, "Hey, fat mama,'' she threw back her head and laughed.

Only Evie seemed uncomfortable there. It was she who planned ahead for the evenings, rinsed her hair in malt vinegar and mourned a broken fingernail and begged Violet not to disgrace her by wearing her wiglet. Yet in the Unicorn she sat slumped behind her beer, chewing her thumb and scowling. She turned often to study the faces of other customers, especially when Drumstrings Casey was playing. Who was that blond who hushed everyone as soon as Casey came on the platform? Wouldn't you know that Evie could never have anything for herself without a lot of other people butting in and certain to win in the end? As if her coming here were a mysterious sort of publicity, the audience grew larger every Saturday and the clapping louder. "There, you see. I know what's what,'' she told Violet. "Now *everybody's* catching on to him.'' But she didn't look happy about it. She watched with a thoughtful, measuring look on her face when he ruffled a strange girl's hair on the way up to the platform.

"You know I'm late,'' he said. *"Will you let me be?*

"I've listened all night.

"I've pondered all day.

"Faces don't stick with me half as much as names.''

The drummer slammed down on his drums. The music grew louder. Oh, it was that talking out of his that made the difference. He never should have begun it. While he spoke Evie held very still, but afterwards, with her eyes wandering over the room, she said, "What would make him do like that?''

"I kind of like it,'' said Violet, starting her second mug of beer.

"Is he saying something? Is there something underneath it? Is he speaking in code?"

Other girls thought nothing of going straight up to him. They crowded around as soon as a set was done. "Now, how did you ever . . ." "Where did you get . . ." Casey slouched easily with his guitar at his side and looked straight through them. He seemed to think they were part of the program. Meanwhile Evie sat by Fay-Jean's empty chair and drew faces in a ring of beer.

"If I were to get his attention," she told Violet, "it would have to be without thinking of it first. Something that just happened. Can you see me going up with those others? I would be planning it ahead, smoothing down my skirt, tucking in my blouse, saying something memorized that would come out backwards, in a reading tone of voice."

"Oh, he wouldn't notice," Violet said.

"That's exactly what I meant."

One Saturday a redhead who was dancing on the platform stood stock still while Casey did his speaking out. It was only one line.

"If I called your name wrong, would you still say yes?"

When the music crashed down again, the redhead said, "You *bet* I would!" Then she left her partner and pulled Casey around by one shoulder to finish the dance. He danced as he played, laughing. It was the first time Evie had seen him laugh. The sudden breaking up of that smooth olive face made him look unfinished and angular, like someone's comical little brother.

"*There's* how to get his attention," Violet said. "Just give him a yank." But when she turned, she saw that Evie was several tables away by now, pushing toward the ladies' room. The boy at Violet's right said, "Hey, little marshmallow, you're all alone." Violet smiled and poured more beer.

Or was it Josh Ballew they all came for? He swaggered onto the platform with his head down and one fist raised, like a prize fighter. Everybody clapped. Fay-Jean appeared in a man's leather jacket and said, "Will you look at how his hair curls up? Oh, I wish *mine* would do that way."

"Nobody got a right to leave me like you left me," Joseph sang. All of his songs were angry. His voice was furry and dark, roughening on vowels, and he stood very close to the microphone. When he started his second song Fay-Jean said, "Will you listen? Evie Decker can have *six* of Drumstrings Casey. Where'd she go, anyhow?"

"Excused herself," said Violet.

Someone screamed.

Joseph Ballew looked pleased, and twanged two sharp notes on his guitar. Then he lowered it to sing another line. He never did both at once. Behind him a murmuring arose, and the other players began looking around, but Joseph sang on with his eyes closed.

"Who screamed?" Violet asked.

Fay-Jean moved away, her jacket swinging from her shoulders. As soon as she was gone Violet turned back to her beer, but then there was another scream. This time the voice was Fay-Jean's.

"My Lord in heaven, Evie Decker!" she said.

Violet stood up. Joseph Ballew stopped playing. The commotion was in a rear corner, by the door to the ladies' room, but even when Violet had angled her way over there the crowd was too tightly packed for her to see anything.

"Will you let me through?" she said. "What is it? Will you let me through?"

Someone bumped into her from behind. "Police," he said. "Clear the way. *Clear* the way." The crowd divided. Violet passed through, widening the path for the policeman. When she reached the door of the ladies' room she stopped suddenly and rocked backward against the policeman's chest.

"Evie?" she said.

Evie was smiling. Two people supported her, the redhead and a skinny blond girl. They held her in a professional, movie-like way, each with one hand beneath Evie's elbow and one at the small of her back. Evie's face was ridged with vertical strands of blood. There were crimson zigzags across her forehead, dampening her hair. "Evie, what *happened*?" said Violet.

"It's his name," Evie said.

The policeman stepped forward, carrying a small pad of paper and a retractable ball-point pen. He clicked the pen. "Name?" he asked.

"Drumstrings Casey," Evie said.

4

She had cut the letters with a pair of nail scissors.
They ran all the way across her forehead, large and
ragged and Greek-looking because straight lines were
easier to cut: ᴧᙎⳆᗅᙎ . In the emergency room, after
they had swabbed the blood away, there was a silence
lasting several seconds. *"Backwards?"* someone said
finally. It looked as if she were staring out at the letters
from within, from the wrong side of her forehead. Or
maybe she had cut them while facing a mirror. Whatever the reason, Evie wasn't telling. She sat in a white
enameled chair beside an instrument case, her shoulders slumped, the lower part of her face round and blank
and pale beneath the red slashes. Her pudgy feet in their
vinyl sandals were twined around the chair rungs. Beside her stood the policeman who had brought her in,
still curious although he had already taken down the
necessary information; and opposite her, right alongside the doctor and nurse, was Violet. Oh, it would take
more than this to shock Violet. She had ridden with
Evie in the back of the squad car, patting her hand
absently. "Evie Decker, I declare," she said, "I wish
you would tell me—Goodness, will you listen? Sirens.
They're for you." Evie only blinked and watched as the
headlights scraped the edges of a tobacco field. When

30

they drove up to the hospital door she said, "I left my
pocketbook in the ladies' room."

"Oh, don't worry. I'll call about it."

"And then what about your car? And I never paid for
my last beer."

"Don't worry."

The others treated her as if she were unconscious,
resting their hands on her shoulder while they leaned
forward to discuss her. "Is she all *right*?" the nurse
said once, and patted Evie's cheeks sharply, almost
slapping her. "Do you think she's all right?"

The doctor shrugged and filled a hypodermic needle.
"Who knows?" he said. "Damn fool teen-agers. Find
her a room, will you? I'm keeping her the night till I
see her state of mind." The nurse left, and so did the
policeman, still staring backwards over his shoulder as
he closed the door. "Should we have tipped him?" Violet said.

"No," said the doctor. "You might as well call her
family. Does she have a family?"

"Only her father."

"He'll have to be told about this."

So Violet left too, rippling the fingers of one hand at
Evie. "Just be a minute," she said. "Take care."

Evie was the only patient in the emergency room.
The doctor worked in silence, snapping threads just
above her eyes with gloved, dead-feeling hands while
water dripped somewhere behind him. "Casey your
boyfriend?" he asked finally.

"No."

"Who, then?"

"Just a singer."

"Rock-and-roll, I suppose."

"That's right."

"Mmhmm." He snapped another thread. "This is

nothing dangerous, you understand. First-degree cuts. But they're ragged. They'll leave scars. You'll need a good plastic surgeon to get rid of them for you.''

Evie stared at a crease in his white coat.

"You all right?" he asked her.

"Yes, fine."

"Well, I can't think why."

Violet returned, swinging her purse by its long strap so that it jingled against her shins at every step. "Your father's on his way," she said. "I said you had to have a little cut stitched up. Was that what you wanted? I couldn't see just out and out *telling* him." She settled on a stool beside the doctor and arranged her skirt around her. "Would you rather I had?"

Evie shook her head.

"Hold still," said the doctor.

He worked for what might have been hours, snapping threads endlessly and sometimes letting out a long whistling sigh between his teeth. Beside him, Violet twirled on her stool and hummed. A clock over the exit jerked each minute by with a deep, pointed click. When finally the doctor laid a strip of gauze over the stitches, Evie saw that it was nearly midnight. "This sets some kind of record," he said. "Aren't there any singers called Al? or Ed?"

"His first name was Drumstrings," Violet told him.

"Well, then, I suppose she did the best she could." He peeled his gloves off. "You can go home tomorrow, if you're in a normal state. Though what *that* would be—Help her to the nurse's station, would you, miss? Ask for Miss Connolly. I'll talk to her father before I send him in."

"Thank you," Evie said.

"You'd be better off in the Peace Corps," said the doctor.

Evie's room held two white beds, both empty, and a maple dresser with a mirror over it. There was only a nightlight on. When she looked in the mirror she saw a wide dark shadow with a band of startling white across the forehead. She touched the band with one finger. "Oh, look, you get a johnny-coat," Violet said. "Only two ties down the whole back of it, and one of them broken. Shall I bring you fresh clothes to wear home tomorrow? Your father'll never think of it."

"No, he probably won't," Evie said.

She pulled off her clothes, which felt creased and heavy from being worn too long. As she dropped each piece to the floor, Violet fumbled for it in the dark and laid it on a chair. Their movements were slow and soundless—Evie's because she felt awkward, Violet's for no known reason because Violet never felt awkward. When Evie had put the gown on, she climbed into the bed farthest from the window. She sat up against the metal headboard, her hands folded across her stomach.

"They'll bring you breakfast in bed, I suppose," Violet said.

"Does Drumstrings Casey know about this?"

"Well, I'm not sure."

"There was a lot of commotion over it. Wouldn't you think he'd have heard?"

"He wasn't singing then. Joseph Ballew was. *I* don't know."

"Didn't you look?"

"Honestly, Evie, I don't *know*. I was with you. I and the policeman. We were busy taking you out."

"I believe this might be the best thing I've ever done," said Evie. "Something out of character. Definite. Not covered by insurance. I'm just sure it will all work out well."

Violet bent to line up the vinyl sandals beneath the

bed. "Why don't you tell me what you want to wear tomorrow," she said. "I'll stop by your house and pick it up."

"Oh, anything. Skirt and blouse. While I was walking through that crowd with the policeman, I kept thinking of my name: Evie Decker, *me*. Taking something into my own hands for once. I thought, if I had started acting like this a long time ago my whole *life* might've been different."

"Well, *that's* for sure," said Violet. "Anyway. Skirt and blouse. Do you want me to stay till your father comes?"

"No, I guess not. Your family will be wondering where you are."

"All right. See you in the morning."

Violet's shoes made a soft, plodding sound out of the room and down the hall. When the sound had faded Evie pulled the sheets over her and lay on her back, staring at the ceiling. Headlights swung across it in slow white wedges. Some sort of blower beneath her window made a steady rushing noise that turned other noises unreal and distant. Her forehead was a tight, thin sheet. There was only a surface pain, but the tightness gave her the feeling that her skin might split into shallow cracks at any moment. She bridged her forehead with one hand, clamping it inward with her thumb and middle finger to ease the stretch.

"Evie?" her father said.

She lowered her hand and winced toward the lighted door. Her father was a tall black angular silhouette, bent at the waist. He entered with his head leading, just as he entered his classroom while students whispered and passed notes and ignored him. "I brought you some clothes," he said.

"Oh. You did?"

"Don't you need them?"

"Well, Violet was going to bring some."

He reached over to the bureau and turned on a lamp, so that her eyes contracted into a sudden ache. "Is that, does that bandage have to be so big?" he asked her.

"It has to cover my whole forehead."

"All of it?"

She shaded her eyes to look at him. "I thought the doctor had told you," she said.

"He did, yes."

"Do you want to see?"

"Oh, no, that's all right."

"I don't mind." She sat up and undid the gauze, which was fastened by adhesive at both ends, and laid it in her lap. "It's only a flesh wound," she said.

"Yes, he said that. He—" Her father looked for only one second before he dropped his eyes again. "I don't understand," he said.

"It's a singer."

"Yes, I know. Casey. I know."

"You know him?"

"I mean, I know that's what the name is. I never heard of Casey before."

"Oh."

"I never even heard of him."

"Well," said Evie.

Her father bent over the bag at his feet, a shopping bag with string handles. "Clothes," he said. He brought out a blouse, a flowered skirt, and underpants but no bra. Finally he came to a pink frilled bedjacket sent her by an aunt two years ago but never used. He laid it in her lap. Evie picked it up and turned it over, smoothing the frills. "A bedjacket," she said.

"I thought you might need it."

In Evie's stubby hands, the frills seemed fussy and

out of place. A bedjacket must have been what he
brought her mother when Evie was born—something he
had been told was expected of him, along with flowers
and a bottle of cologne. Evie's mother had been the last
woman in Pulqua County to die of childbed fever. Her
father never mentioned her (and never said, "You are
what I traded your mother for, and it was a bad bargain
at that," which was what Evie continually expected to
hear). But the bedjacket, with its satin buttons, seemed
to be giving him away without his realizing it, speaking
up out of all those years of silence. "Well, thank you
very much," Evie said.

He went over to the window, jamming his hands into
his pockets. Everything about him was long and bony;
nothing but his awkwardness had been passed on to
Evie. His hair and lashes were pale, his eyes set in deep
shadowed sockets, his skin sprinkled with large freckles
so faint that they seemed to be seeping through a white
over-layer. "Plastic surgeons take money, of course—"
he was saying.

"I don't want one."

He barely heard her. His mind had snagged on a new
thought. "Evie, had you been drinking?" he asked.
"Was that it?"

"Half a beer."

"But then, why would you do it?"

Evie spread her fingers in front of her and studied
them like a deck of cards while she chose her words.
"Now, I'm not trying to be rude," she said finally,
"but it *was* my face. It is. It's my business how it
looks."

"You'd feel awfully silly with 'Casey' across your
forehead all your life."

"I'd feel sillier having it erased the day after I did
it," said Evie.

"Well, that's the worst of it. You *can't* erase it the next day, you have to wait until it heals. Could you maybe cut bangs, meanwhile?"

"No," said Evie.

Her father rubbed the pouches under his eyes, smoothing and re-pleating them. "Evie, honey," he said. "There are *plenty* of nice boys in the world. Just give yourself time. You're a sweet-looking girl, after all, and when you lose a—when you're older, boys are going to fall all over themselves for you, take my word. You're only sixteen now."

"Seventeen," said Evie.

"Seventeen. So why should you ruin your life for some singer in a roadhouse? Listen. The doctor's giving you a tranquilizer. You have a good night's sleep, and tomorrow I'll come get you and we'll talk it over. Things will look different in the morning. You'll see."

Evie said nothing. She rolled the strip of gauze into a small cylinder.

"Well, good night, Evie."

He clicked off the lamp. Then at the door he stopped and turned. "Another thing," he said. "Tell that Casey boy not to bother coming around again. I won't allow you to see any more of him."

Evie looked up, with two small pleased folds beginning at the outer corners of her eyes. But by then he had jammed his hands back in his pockets and walked away.

They gave her some sort of pill but she spent a bad night anyway, tossing beneath a light, frowning sleep. Strange beds bothered her. Splinters of dreams came and went, leaving only echoes of themselves to remember in the morning. And when she awoke, all her muscles ached. She sat up and looked out toward the corridor, where specks of sunlight floated slowly above the polished red floor. "Nurse!" she tried. No one answered.

Somewhere in her waking, the thought of her forehead floated by like yesterday's surprise, some new possession which would have to be confirmed again today. She slid off the high bed and padded over to the bureau mirror, keeping her nightgown hitched shut behind her.

Her forehead was an angry doll's, crisscrossed with black stitches. The word "Casey," reflected right side around, formed itself only after several seconds, during which she stood stunned and motionless with her mouth barely open. Later, maybe, it would be immediately legible. But today the threads turned her forehead first into a jagged design, a grayish-white crazy-quilt covering the space between her hairline and her straight brown eyebrows, which were flaked with dried blood. All her other features seemed to have drained away. Her lips were pale, and her eyes had lightened. Her nose looked flatter. For years she had cherished the few surprises hidden away in her shapelessness: a narrow nose, slender wrists, and perfect oval fingernails. Now, still looking into the mirror, she held up both wrists and turned the blue-veined, glistening insides of them toward the glass. Then she backed away, very slowly. But when she was as far as she could get, pressed against the wall behind her, the letters still stood out ragged and black. "Casey." A voice inside her read the name out, coolly: "Casey."

Something on wheels was coming down the hallway. Evie climbed back into bed and sat there, with her wrists still upturned in her lap, while her heart began thudding at an uneven rate. There was no way she could steady it. She breathed deeply, gazed at a blank wall, straightened her back. Her heart kept racing and then pausing, collecting itself to race again.

A nurse wheeled in a cart laid with pills in paper cups and a jarful of thermometers. "*Here* we are," she said. She looked over at Evie, with a thermometer in mid-air, and opened her mouth but said nothing. Her face had the same pale, startled look that Evie's had had in the mirror. But when she spoke again all she said was, "Have a nice night?" She slid the thermometer into Evie's mouth and reached for a wrist. Evie was too intent on her heartbeat to answer. She went on staring at the wall, keeping her lips conscientiously tight around the thermometer. In a minute, now, the nurse would know from her pulse that something was wrong. She would drop the wrist and run to fetch doctors, oxygen tents, digitalis—taking the responsibility from Evie, letting her rest finally while someone else steadied her heartbeat. But when the minute was up, the nurse had still said nothing. Evie stopped looking at the wall. She found the nurse's eyes just brushing her, very briefly, and then settling on the thermometer which she plucked out and shook down with no more than a glance at it. "Breakfast'll be along," she said. She set the thermometer on a paper napkin and wheeled the cart out.

If she lay still, Evie kept hearing the blood thudding unevenly through her ears. She drowned the sound by struggling out of bed, trailing one sheet halfway across the floor and limping on the foot that was tangled in the sheet's folds. Her hospital gown bellied out like a sail when she bent to free herself. Her hair fell forward in dark, rigid strings, matted with blood. After she had kicked the door shut she dressed in a flurry of deliberate noises: clicking snaps, shuffling sandals, slamming drawers as she looked through the bureau for a stray comb. All she found were a box of Wipettes and a booklet called "Our Daily Bread." She shut the final drawer and then raised her head, listening. Her heartbeat was regular again. Or if not regular, at least unnoticeable. In the mirror a steady pulse quivered one point of her collar, and a black-pointed design was plastered above it like a label.

After breakfast, a nurse's aide appeared in the doorway and folded her hands across her pinafore. "Photographer's coming," she said. "You're going to be famous."

Evie sat on the foot of her bed, snapping her watchband over and over and waiting for someone to remember she was there. "Famous?" she said. "What? Photographer?"

"They heard what you did," said the nurse's aide. She spun out of the room. Just before she disappeared she remembered to say, "That singer guy, too. He's coming."

"What singer?"

"Yezac."

Evie got off the bed. It was better to be standing. No, sitting. But there was no place to sit except the bed, whose sheets were still strung out across the room. She stood in the middle of the floor with her hands clasped behind her, straight-armed, shifting from one foot to another. She felt like a package at a post office, stamped and addressed, and the heel-taps of the addressee were clicking closer and closer down the hall. She could hear him clearly now. She heard how the swing in his walk created silences between his steps: click, space, click, while whoever was with him luff-luffed steadily along in soft-soled shoes. The photographer, a small bald man hung with several strapped objects, arrived in the doorway first. "Paul Ogle, Pulqua *Times*," he said. Then he crossed the room to the far corner, holding a light meter to Evie's chin on the way. And there, finally, came Drumstrings Casey. He wore his black denim and his high leather boots. He had on sunglasses made of a silvery black that mirrored Evie perfectly and turned his own face, what you could see of it, into something as hard and as opaque as the glasses themselves. "Shades off, Casey," the photographer said. "I want a reaction."

Drumstrings Casey leaned against the doorframe, crossed one boot, and removed his sunglasses. His face lost its smoothness. He had, after all, the narrow brown eyes that Evie expected, so straight-edged that each seemed formed from a pair of parallel lines. The slant of hair was not greased down today; he ruffled it through his fingers, stroking his forehead with the same motion. "It's the newspaper lady," he said.

"No," said Evie. She meant no, she was not from the newspaper at all and had told him so before; but Casey, misunderstanding, said, "Well, you sure do look like her."

"More reaction, Casey," the photographer said. Casey stretched his mouth wide into a wide straight line. "Will you turn this way, miss?" Evie turned, focusing her eyes upon a drawer-pull for as long as she felt Casey watching. The photographer clicked the shutter. "Now, Casey, put your arm around her. Smile. Don't you know how to smile?" But Casey only stared fixedly at the bottom half of Evie's face. Every now and then his eyes darted up to her forehead and then down again, as if they had run away with him for a second. Across Evie's shoulders his arm was limp and motionless, the hand falling open off the edge of her sleeve. He had the pleasantly bitter smell of marigolds. Even this close, he seemed filmed by cold air.

The camera clicked again. For the first time, Evie
remembered that the purse she had left at the Unicorn
contained her snapshot of Drumstrings Casey. "Oh—"
she said, but when the two men turned, she went back
to staring at the drawer-pull. The snapshot had come
out dappled by tiny pools of light, glinting for no ap-
parent reason on the edges of his dark clothes and on
his face, which was tilted slightly up, the veiled eyes
turned in her direction.

"Now, it's Evie, that right? Evie Decker," said the
photographer. He was writing on a scrap of paper with
bitten-looking edges. "Age?"

"Seventeen."

"Seventeen. Really? Occupation?"

"I go to school."

"I thought you were older," the photographer said.
"Now. Could you tell me what end you had in mind?"

"End?"

"What your goal was in doing this?"

"Oh," said Evie.

"Your reason, then. Could you tell me your reason?"

Drumstrings Casey shifted his weight, his fingers
hooked in his back pockets.

"Let's put it this way," the photographer said. "We'll
say you're just a music fan. You dig rock, especially
Casey's rock. That sound about right?"

"Oh, well, I guess so."

"We'll put it in quotes, then. Now, would you mind
telling what you did it with?"

"I don't remember," said Evie, suddenly tired.

"Was it all of a sudden? Had you planned it?"

"It's hard to say."

"Well, I suppose that's enough," the photographer
said. "It's only going to be a caption."

Drumstrings Casey straightened up. "A caption, what's that?" he asked.

"The writing under a photo. *You* know."

"Couldn't you give it more?"

"It's not *me* that says, boy, it's the boss."

"Well, God almighty," Casey said.

"What now?"

"Wasn't it you that was waking me at seven this morning? Shouting about publicity? I don't see what *that* was all about. Little old grainy newspaper picture, heap of gray dots nobody'll recognize."

"Don't talk to me, talk to your drummer," said the photographer. "He's the one called *me*. Well, thanks, folks." And out he walked, leaving the two of them alone in the middle of the room.

"Well," said Casey. He slipped his dark glasses back on and jammed his shirt down tighter into his pants. Then he turned toward Evie. Behind the glasses it was hard to tell where he was looking. "What'd you go and cut it backwards for?" he asked her.

"It just worked out that way," said Evie.

"Worked out that way, how do you mean?"

"I don't know, that's just the way it happened. Can't you read it?"

"Sure, I can read it."

"Now I can see that it's uneven," Evie said. "I know that's going to bother me. Every time I look in a mirror I'll think, why did I let the Y droop? Why did I shake on the C?"

"Why did you make it 'Casey'?" Casey said.

She stared, mistaking his meaning. She thought he had asked the only question she minded answering.

"Why not my first name?" he asked. "There're thousands of Caseys around."

"What, *Drumstrings*? I don't have that big of a forehead."

"Drum," he said. "Nobody says the whole thing,
for Lord's sake."

"They call you Drum?" asked Evie.

"That's right."

"Well, I certainly wish I'd of known."

"Yeah, I suppose it's too late now," he said.

He was teetering on his heels, his hands in his back
pockets again, plainly thinking of going. Evie pressed
her palms together and said, "You are going to be famous someday."

He raised his sunglasses to stare at her. His eyes were
bleached-looking in the sudden light. "It's funny," he
said finally. "I would never have took you for a rock
fan at all." Evie held still under his gaze, until he
dropped the glasses and turned toward the door. "Certainly was a peculiar feeling," he said to nobody special. "Feels like meeting up with your own face
somewhere." He was halfway out the door now, but
still with no good-byes, no summing up, no rounding
off of the conversation before he left. "Almost like
something you would dream in bed at night," he said,
but by then he was out of sight. His voice was sliding
away and his boots were ambling down the hall. Evie
remained where she was for several minutes, staring out
the open doorway. She was used to definite endings.
When Drum Casey left he trailed bits of conversation
like wisps from a cotton ball, clouding the air behind
him. His voice remained in the hall, disembodied. His
heel-taps clicked for a long time without seeming to get
farther away. The doctor when he came found Evie
alone in the middle of her room, surveying the insides
of her wrists, and he shook his head and signed her
discharge papers in silence.

5

Messes rose up wherever she sat; that was the kind of mood she was in. For days after she came home from the hospital, she stayed in a draggled bathrobe, as if she were truly an invalid, while clutter collected magically in an oval around her chair. Flakes of lint speckled the rug. Candy papers overflowed the ash trays. The slipcover sagged on the chair cushion and grew creased and dingy. Yet from morning to night Evie hardly moved, just sat on the back of her neck with her arms limp at her sides and an open magazine in her lap. Clotelia, passing through the living room, jabbed a broom under Evie's legs. "Excuse, please. Move," she said. Evie frowned at the broom and picked a chocolate out of the box at her elbow.

People called to ask about her. Not classmates, but friends of her father's. "*You* talk to them," Evie told Clotelia. She heard conversations from outdoors, at twilight, while her father was sprinkling the lawn. "Evening, Sam. Is Evie, I hear she had a little accident. Or rather—" "Go on now," someone said, "they tell me that girl of yours has slashed her wrists with a movie star's initials. Is that true?" "Forehead," said her father. "A singer. His full last name." When he came in, his face would be pouched and sagging. Grownups wearing that expression usually said, when asked, "No,

not angry. Just disappointed.'' Only Evie never asked
and her father never said it, not out loud.

She covered her forehead with gauze from the medicine cabinet and taped it at both ends, the way the
doctor had. Her hair, which she still had not washed,
remained stiff with blood in front and limp and damp-
looking behind. She wore a bathrobe faded from sky
blue to gray, grayer along the edges, and her slippers
were gray too, a matted pile that had started out white.
Even without the mysterious clutter around her, any
corner she inhabited would still have seemed untidy.
"You are a sight," Clotelia said. "You constituting a
mess all by your lone self." Evie only stared at her and
turned a page of her magazine.

Her teachers sent her assignments home with her father. At first her father seemed relieved that she was
staying out of school. In the mornings as he left he said,
"That's the girl. You just take it easy a while, I'll see
you tonight." But it was clear that he expected things
to fall into some sort of progression—the blood to be
washed from her hair, the gauze removed, bangs cut.
Evie took no steps at all. Toward the end of the week
she kept an appointment to have her stitches out, but
then she came home and got back into her bathrobe.
Let's see you,'' her father said that evening. Evie tilted
her face up, exposing a naked forehead with "Casey"
running across it in dried red dots. "Ah, yes," said her
father. He looked away again.

She rose every morning just as he left for work, and
drank a glass of orange juice in her easy chair. Then
she opened a magazine. Her father bought her magazines at a newsstand, carefully choosing those which
had nothing to do with rock music, or teen-agers, or
even love. If she was not in a reading mood she held
one of his selections open on her lap while she stared

into space, but when she got bored she dove under the skirt of the chair for what Clotelia read: *Jet, Ebony,* and *Revealing Romances*. She chewed a fingernail and raced through vague, hopeful confession stories and smeared advertisements for hair straighteners and bust creams. By then Clotelia would be making passes at the living room with a dirty dustcloth. "What you read that trash for?" she asked Evie. "You know it only snarl your mind."

"I want to see where you get your outlook on life," Evie said.

Clotelia emptied one wastebasket into another, piece by piece.

Clotelia's skin was a pale cocoa, but since she had started dating Brewster Miggs she called herself black and wore her hair in a bush. "Brewster don't want me doing day-work no more, either," she told Evie. "Say I got to quit. I tell him I will." Yet she continued to show up every morning, at nine or nine-thirty or ten, wearing ski pants and an African cape. When she chose to do any cleaning she kept up a running conversation with the dirt. "Come out of there, you. I see you. How come you to bug me this way? That's all this house is, filth. Filth."

"You should know," said Evie. She felt continually disappointed by Clotelia. Four years, and Clotelia was still an indifferent stranger kicking dust puffs with the toe of a cream suede high-heeled boot. Other people would have turned into members of the family by now. Clotelia carried her purse with her from room to room all day long, and massaged pink lotion into her hands while staring out the kitchen window. When she poked a mop beneath a radiator, Evie felt that the whole house was suffering from some sort of disdain. It was such a leaden, damp-smelling house. The flowered furniture

and lacy figurines had sat so long in their places that
they seemed to have jelled there, hardening around the
edges. Clotelia passed among them scornfully, with
earrings as big as slave bands flashing knives of light
across the walls.

At noon, when the soap operas came on, Clotelia
always settled before the television with her feet outstretched and a beer between her knees. "Clotelia,
where is lunch?" Evie asked.

"I'm watching the stories now."

"Well, I see you are."

"Something happen to your feet?"

"I just did get home from the hospital," Evie said.

"What, was it your feet give you trouble? No sir.
Your head." She tapped her temple and went back to
watching "Love of Life." Evie wouldn't have eaten
lunch anyway. She ate chocolates, or the last of a pack
of Nabs in Clotelia's purse. Meanwhile the soap operas
toiled on, one after the other. People quarreled and
sobbed and flung out of rooms to organ music, and Evie
kept saying, "Oh, for—" but watching, anyway, caught
up in what was going on. Clotelia talked about the char-
acters as if they were relatives. "I don't know what *she*
doing. That boy don't care two flicks for her. You ever
seen her mother? Talk about nosy. At Chistmastime she
trail that girl all the way to New York, that's where she
went for the holidays, and eagle-eyed? Oh, she give me
the creeps. I despise a woman to be that way."

"She's got no sense of privacy," said Evie, crum-
pling the Nabs wrapper.

"Oh, don't tell *me*. You remember when her boy got
engaged?"

"I didn't see it."

"Well, it was to a sweet girl but I wasn't easy about
her. Something she was hiding. Naturally his mother

saw it right off. She don't miss a trick. Stop wagging your foot, will you? Like to driving me crazy.''

"It's all I've got to do," said Evie, but she stilled her foot.

"Every time I get out of here Brewster say, 'Honey, why you so *evil* today? I never seen you so evil.' I say, 'It's that Evie. She driving me crazy,' I say.''

"I don't do one thing to you," Evie said.

"Oh, no? Look at you, wherever you sit you just causing a shambles. I already cleaned that space today. Will you look at it?''

Evie looked. Crumpled cellophane lay beside her chair, and cheese cracker crumbs littered her lap and the rug. "What do you expect?" she said. "I just came out of the hospital.''

"Hospital is right. And you be right back in, if you don't rise off that fat butt of yours. You hear what happen if you sit too long?''

"What.''

"You bust your skin seams. You pop right open, you leak out the cracks.''

Clotelia never would act the way she was supposed to.

After school Violet would stop by. She carried her books and all the odds and ends she had accumulated during the day—someone's broken looseleaf binder, blank newsprint from the journal office, a tissue flower found in a wastebasket. She saved things. She saved bits of gossip she had heard third-hand, so far removed from the outer circle she and Evie inhabited that sometimes even the names were missing. "You know that real tall cheerleader? The one that does the split after the fight song? She had to get married. Lola Nesbitt has fought with that boy she dates. I saw him send a note into her class and hang around outside waiting for her to read it, but she never did.''

Pulled from one set of plots into another, Evie frowned at the television set and tried to collect her thoughts. ''Is he the one that debates?'' she said.

''I think so. Miss Ogden is back from her honeymoon. She's Mrs. Bishop now. Has a florentined wedding-ring set with diamond chips. It looks kind of tacky; everybody says so.''

''What do they say about me?'' Evie asked.

''Oh, well, I don't know.''

''They don't say anything?''

''Well, bits and pieces. *You* know.''

On the television screen a tense married couple sat gingerly circling each other's feelings, casting significant looks after a simple sentence, causing the music to swell ominously over no more than a phrase and a pair of lowered eyes. Violet watched them and tapped a fingernail against her front teeth.

''My father thinks I'm going to a plastic surgeon,'' Evie said.

''Well, aren't you?''

''Ha,'' said Clotelia. ''You think she got that much sense?''

''I don't know yet,'' Evie said, ''but I doubt if I am.''

''You could cut bangs.''

''That would be worse. Showing up at school wearing bangs all of a sudden, everyone knowing why.''

''Then go to the surgeon.''

''Watch, now,'' Clotelia said. ''This man here is some operator. Listen to his sweet-talk. Yesterday he was after that blond, the one before the commercial. Fickle?''

"I'm not sorry the letters are *there*," Evie said. "I'm glad. I'm talking about something else."

"What, then?"

"Well, I don't really know."

"School will be out in just a few more weeks anyhow," said Violet.

"I keep forgetting."

"That's because you don't get outdoors. It's hot now."

"Is it?" Evie twisted in her seat, tearing a shank of hair through her fingers. "I just hate summer," she said.

"Every year you tell me that."

"I mean it. What have I got to look forward to? You know what I thought, Violet: This summer might be different. Now it looks like it won't be."

"Why would it be different?"

Evie didn't answer, but Clotelia did. "Ha. Thought that Casey boy would come riding up and spirit her away, once he heard what she done."

"You hush," said Evie.

"I don't see him beating down no doors. Do you?"

"Ignore her," Evie told Violet.

Violet sighed and wrapped her hands around each other. "You could take your finals at home," she said. "Your father could arrange it."

"You think I'm scared to go back."

"Well, Evie, here you *sit*. What are you staying around home for?"

"Look. Can't you tell me what they're all saying? I won't care. I promise I won't. Just tell me what you've heard."

"I already did," said Violet. "Just bits and pieces, that's all. Someone will come up and say, 'Is it true what I heard about that friend of yours?' 'What'd you hear?' I say, and they say, 'Oh, *you* know.' ''

"But you must have to answer sometime," Evie said. "What do you tell them?"

"I tell them yes, I believe there *was* something like that."

"Do they act surprised?"

"What would they act surprised for? If they asked, they must have already known."

"Well, shocked then. Do they laugh? What do they *say*?"

"Oh, they just think a while. Like when—but no, not exactly—"

"Like when."

"Like when the cheerleader had to get married, I was going to say."

"They think I did something evil, then."

"No, I didn't mean that. Good Lord. Like when someone has crossed over where the rest of them haven't been. Getting pregnant, or dying, or that boy in the band who shot himself. Remember that? You think, 'Why, I saw him in the hallway, often. And sat behind him in algebra. But I never *knew*, and now he has gone and done it.' That's what they sound like."

"Ah," said Evie.

At suppertime, Evie and her father sat opposite each other at the tiny kitchen table. Clotelia would have set out the food and left by then, slamming the front door behind her and clicking away down the sidewalk. She rarely said good-bye. The silence she left behind seemed an angry one, as if she had said, "Now, you've done it. See? I'm leaving. I've had all I can take." The two of them looked guilty and awkward as they sat poking their baked beans. "*Well*, now," her father would say finally. "Tell me what you've done with yourself today.

Talked to anyone? Been out much?'' But all Evie ever answered was, "I didn't see anyone. I didn't go anywhere."

"Violet come over?"

"Yes."

"How was she?"

"Oh, fine."

His impatience was controlled, showing up only in the way he fidgeted with a fork or drank water in deep, hasty gulps. He did no reading at the table nowadays. He concentrated solely on Evie, as if he had made some sort of resolution. When Evie tried to keep on reading herself, she felt his eyes on her and his premeditated smile, burdening her mind until she had to give up and shove the magazine aside. "All right," she would tell him.

"What?"

"Was there something you wanted to say?"

"Why, no. Not that I can think of."

They finished the meal without speaking, every clink of fork against plate sounding as loud and as artificial as a sound effect. Food she didn't enjoy, Evie thought, was not fattening. She waded through her mound of baked beans and frankfurters, lukewarm rings of canned pineapple and instant mashed potatoes, and everything sank heavily to her stomach and left her feeling uncomfortable but virtuous. When her father brought sherbet glasses full of Jello from the refrigerator, she ate every last mouthful and set her spoon down neatly beside her knife. Then they were free. They could go off to opposite ends of the house and do whatever kept them busy.

She no longer listened to the radio. She lay on her bed filing her fingernails or leafing through more magazines, and sometimes she fell into daydreams that involved one-sided, whispered conversations. "Aren't you Drum Casey? I thought you were. I heard you sing once, years ago. Yes, I'm Evie Decker. I was fat back then, I didn't think you would recognize me." She would toss her hair back, exposing a smooth white forehead. But not surgically smooth. She pictured the effects of plastic surgery as being just that, plastic, a white poreless rectangle like a blank label surrounded on four sides by a thin border of scar tissue. In her daydream, the smoothness was natural and the ragged letters spelling "Casey" would have been only a joke, something she had written in red ink as a prank or, better yet, just something Casey had made up. "Letters, you say? I never cut letters. Where did you get *that* idea? Do you think I go around cutting strange names in my face?"

But she always ended up feeling hopeless and betrayed. Rising to fetch a Kleenex or an emery board, she would catch sight of her reflection whispering in the bureau mirror and she would clamp her lips shut and lie down again. Then by nine o'clock she would have started trying to sleep. All her muscles lay coiled from a day of sitting. She turned from one side to another, tightening her sheet over and over in order to erase the untidy feeling that followed her even to bed.

On Tuesday morning, ten days after she had returned from the hospital, her father said, "Evie, honey, I'd like to talk to you."

"Hmm?" said Evie. She was already in her easy chair, a bag of marshmallows beside her.

"I was wondering about school. Don't you feel like going back now?"

"Oh. Well, no, I don't," Evie said. She looked up at her father, who stood rocking gently above her. The morning sunlight bleached the tips of his lashes. "I'm not really up to it yet," she told him.

"Up to it? What do you mean?"

"Well, I believe I have a low-grade virus. I would go back otherwise, but I think I should stay out till I'm well. My head aches."

"But if that's all—"

"And my stomach's upset. My joints are stiff."

"Evie, honey, the school has made quite a few allowances for you. With finals so near—"

"Well, maybe tomorrow," Evie said.

"Do you mean that?"

"Sure."

But when he went he paused at the door for a moment, jingling his keys, and the silence behind him left Evie with a suspended feeling.

She sat very still for a long time, staring into space with her hands in her lap. A clock struck. A lawnmower started up. Clotelia banged the front door and went straight to the kitchen to make coffee, showing Evie nothing but the back of a swirling cape. "Clotelia!" Evie called.

Clotelia didn't answer.

"*Clotelia!*"

But there was only the rattling of cutlery.

Evie waited a minute longer, and then she heaved herself out of her chair and went over to the hall telephone. Dust outlined the directory beside it. She thumbed through the pages until she came to the listings for Farinia: a page and a half of names, mostly Frazells. There were three people named Casey. The first was Asquith, which didn't sound likely. Then there was a B.L., and after that an Obed E. If his father's name were B. for Bertram, wouldn't Drum have to be called Bertram junior? She dialed the number anyway. A woman answered, out of breath. "Hello," said Evie. "May I speak to Drum?"

"Who?"

"Drumstrings."

There was a silence.

"Bertram?" Evie said.

"Who?"

"Well, I must have the wrong number."

"I reckon you must."

The woman hung up. Evie pressed the dial tone and then called Obed E., where another woman answered.

"Yes, hello."

"I'd like to speak to Drum, please," Evie said.

"To—Oh." The receiver at the other end clattered against something, and the woman called, "Bertram? Phone." Evie stood hunched over the tall table, clutching folds of bathrobe to her stomach.

"Hello," Drum Casey said.

"This is Evie Decker."

"Huh?"

"I carved your name on my forehead."

"*Oh*, yes," said Drum. He seemed to be eating something; he chewed and swallowed.

"I was wondering if I could see you for a minute."

"Oh," Drum said. "Well. . . ."

"It'll only take a second. There's something I wanted to discuss with you."

"What's that?"

"I'll have to tell you when I see you. Will you come over?"

"I'm in Farinia," said Drum.

"I know you are. Don't you have a car?"

"Look. What do you think, my wire is tapped? Just tell me on the phone, why don't you."

"It would be to your advantage," Evie said. Her speech seemed to be turning formal. To make up for it she said, "No skin off *my* neck."

"Well, wait a minute," said Drum. She heard him farther off, calling, "Mom?" It stunned her to think of Drum Casey as someone's son, part of a family, possessing even an age which she had never thought to wonder about. When he came back he said, "Okay. Where you at?"

"I'm at home."

"Where's *that*?"

"Fourteen-twenty Hawthorne."

"Now, you sure you can't say this over the phone."

"I'm positive," said Evie.

When she hung up she found Clotelia right behind her, holding a cup of coffee and shaking her head. "*Oh, Evie*," she said. "What call you got to act so ignorant?"

Evie turned and went upstairs without answering.

Nothing was fit to wear. She didn't have a single dress she could stand, and she went through her closet flailing at skirts and jingling hangers. Finally she settled on a red taffeta party dress. Its hem was far too long for this year or even last year, but at least it was red. She slipped it over her head and tugged until the buttons met the buttonholes. Then she put on her vinyl sandals. In the bathroom, she bent over the sink to wash her hair with a bar of Ivory. It was lucky she had not cut bangs. Her hair lay plastered to her skull in dark wet lines from an almost central part, and coiled into snaky circles at her jaws. Freckles that were usually invisible stood out clearly on her pale skin, more dots of red echoing the dots above. She smiled in the mirror, exposing large square teeth. She frowned and turned away.

While she waited on the front porch, clutching her books to her chest, disapproval hung like a fog up and down her street. A lady in a gardening hat clipped her hedge, throwing Evie sharp, sidelong looks with every

snick of her shears. Blank-faced houses watched her
sternly. Behind her, in her own house, Clotelia slammed
doors and shoved furniture and muttered to herself, although Evie couldn't hear what it was she said. Once
she came to stand behind the screen with a crane-necked
watering pitcher in her hand. "I've a good mind to call
your daddy," she told Evie.

"What would you tell him?"

"You know he don't want you seeing that trash."

"I'm not doing anything wrong," said Evie. She
straightened, throwing a sudden smile at the gardening
lady. Her father had banned Drum Casey as if Drum
were storming the front hedge, bearing flowers and a
ladder, begging to be let in. She could almost pretend
that her father knew something she didn't. But when
finally Drum drove up, in a battered black Dodge with
upside-down license plates, all he did was lean out his
window and give her a long, unsmiling stare. Evie
hugged her books tighter and started toward him.

"You going somewhere?" he asked.

"I have to get to school. I thought you could drive
me there while we were talking."

"Funny time to go to school."

"I know. I'm late."

She opened the car door and climbed in beside him.
The car had a hot, syrupy smell in the morning sunlight. Instead of the black denim that he sang in, Drum
Casey wore blue jeans and a T shirt with sleeves rolled
up past his biceps. The soft colors gave him a gentler,
faded look. He was leaning on the steering wheel, the
shock of hair falling forward over his face. He slid his
eyes past her forehead without ever quite looking at it.
"I ain't got much time," he said.

Evie only smiled. "I thought you might have a motorcycle," she told him.

"Me, a bike?"

"A motorcycle."

"Naw, they're too dangerous."

"Oh, I see," said Evie. She watched Drum set the car into motion, steering easily with his forearms resting on the wheel. He wore a wristwatch with a silver expansion band, which gave her a smaller version of the shock she had felt when she heard him call his mother. Did he wind his watch every morning, check its accuracy, try to be places on time like ordinary people? "How old are you?" she asked him.

"Nineteen."

"I'm seventeen."

Drum said nothing.

"If you're nineteen," said Evie, "do you go to school?"

"No."

"What, then."

"I don't do much of nothing."

"Oh."

The car turned onto Main Street. They passed a clutter of small shops and cafés, the bowling alley and the Christian Science Reading Room. Evie pressed tight against the window, but there was nobody to see her.

"What was it you wanted to tell me?" Drum asked.

"Well, I had an idea this morning."

"Is this where I turn?"

"No, one block farther."

"Only been here once before, but I'm good at directions."

"We got written up in the paper. Did you see it?" Evie asked.

"Yeah, I saw it. Just a picture, though."

"Well, it's better than nothing."

"Sure."

"Somebody sent me a copy in the mail." She rummaged through her notebook until she had found it: a plastic-sealed photograph of her in her hospital room, rising from a wave of strung-out sheets, and Drum scowling beside her. Taped to the plastic was a printed message. "Congratulations on your recent achievement. And when it's the *tops* in achievement you want, just think of Sonny Martin, Pulqua Country's Biggest Real Estate Agent." "This rightly belongs to you," Evie said. "Here. Keep it." Drum took his eyes from the road a minute to glance at it, and then he nodded and put it into his back pocket.

"Thanks," he said.

"It's good publicity."

"Sure, I reckon."

"How do you usually get publicity?" she asked him.

Drum gave a sudden short laugh, as if it had been startled out of him. "Well, not *that* way," he said.

"Do you put in ads?"

"I got a manager."

"Oh. I thought only fighters had managers."

"Well, no," said Drum. "Well, them too, of course." He had drawn up before the school by now but sat frowning, tapping one finger on the wheel, as if he were no longer sure that a manager was what he had. "Of course, he's only my drummer," he said finally.

"Does he put in ads?"

"Sometimes. Or talks around, mostly. Goes to see people."

"Wouldn't he like it if you got more publicity?"

"What you getting at?"

"I was thinking if I started coming to all your shows, where people could see me. Wearing my hair off my face. Wouldn't it cause talk? They'd say, 'You see what

she did for him. There must be something to him, then.'
Wouldn't they?''

"Oh, I reckon," said Drum. "Until you got healed
up."

"Healed up? What are you talking about? *I'm* not
going to get healed up."

He didn't react the way she had expected. He stopped
tapping his fingers and slumped back in his seat, staring
at the windshield. After a minute he said, *"What?"*

"I thought you knew."

"Are you going to have, um—"

"Scars," said Evie.

A line of girls in gym shorts crossed the playing field,
followed by Drum's darkened eyes. "Jesus," he said.

"Well, it's done now. Wouldn't you like to have me
sitting there while you played? People would say, 'We
better go hear Drum Casey, there's this girl who cut—' ''

"Are you out of our head?"

"Why? What's so crazy about that?"

"For you, maybe nothing," said Drum. "But I ain't
going to sing under those conditions."

"What conditions?"

"How do you think I would feel?"

"Well, I don't see—"

"Go on, now," said Drum. "Get out. I'm real sorry
about what happened, but I got my own life to live."

"Nobody said you didn't."

"Will you *go*?"

"You can live your own life all you want," said Evie,
but she could feel her words fading away from her.
Drum had reached across her to open the car door. His
arm was covered with fine brown hairs, dotted with the
faintest sheen of sweat, and for one motionless second
she stared down and mourned it, just that isolated arm
which she had only now started to know. Then she said,

"All right. If that's the way you feel." She stumbled out onto the sidewalk, clutching at slipping books and smoothing the back of her rumpled skirt. Her face felt heavy, as if some weight at her jawline were pulling all her features downward.

Yet when she started up the front steps of the school, two girls in gym shorts were staring past her at the disappearing Dodge. They looked at her, then at the Dodge again. Evie smiled at them and went inside. If two people saw, the whole school would know by noon. They would pass it from desk to desk and down the lunchline: "That girl who slashed the singer's name in her face, well, now she's hanging out with him. He drove her to school. Sat a long time in the car with her. What were they doing in the car?"

She smiled at a boy she didn't know and set her books down in front of her locker. If the boy stared at her forehead, she didn't notice. The letters stood out clear and proud, framed by damp hair, finer than any plastic rectangle a surgeon could have pasted there.

6

Drum Casey's drummer's name was David Elliott. Some people had tried calling him "Guitar" for a joke, just rounding things off, but David was the kind who slid out from under nicknames. He was not light-minded enough. He played the drums intently, watching his hands, sitting very straight instead of hunkering over the way other drummers did. This made him seem childlike, although he was a good six feet tall. He had white-blond hair that fell in an even line, hiding his eyebrows. His face was fine-boned and his eyes transparent, the color of old blue Mason jars. Yet girls never took to him. They liked his looks but not his seriousness. He spoke too definitely; there was a constant, edgy impatience in the way he moved, and he planned ahead too much. "We're good. We're going good," he told girls. "I want to hit a night club next. We're getting up there. We're ready to move." Drum, beside him, was slow and cool and dark. He made plans too; but while David talked about up, Drum talked about out. "When we get out of this place, I want me a custom car. Going to go so far I'll lose the way home, forget the name of the town, mislay the map. Also new singing clothes; I want me something shiny." Girls understood what he meant. They fluttered after him when he drifted off, and David stayed behind to think up more publicity.

David solicited clubs and roadhouses and church organizations. During the day he sold insurance policies door to door, but he never forgot to work the conversation around to music. "Spring is here. Are you going to have a dance? Do you know of any dances? You'll need a band, records aren't the same. What about Mrs. Howard, the one in the house on the hill? She gives a dance every May. Won't she need a band? Ask her. It's cheaper to hire the two of us; those big groups can get out of hand." He believed in gimmicks, little eye-catching traps for people to fall into while they were making up their minds. Bright red cards with gilt lettering on them—"Drumstrings with guitar, David with the sticks, 839–3036"—were thumbtacked to every bulletin board. David's Jeep was painted with psychedelic swirls and a purple telephone number. In December, he had sent Christmas cards picturing an orchestra of angels to every leading businessman in Pulqua, Farinia, and Tar City. He instructed Drum to carry his guitar slung over his shoulder at all times, but Drum didn't. ("In the *pharmacy*?" Drum said. "At the liquor store? You're putting me on.") And when Evie Decker slashed "Casey" across her forehead, it was David who called the newspaper photographer. "This is why you need a manager," he told Drum. "Would you have thought of it by yourself? You haven't got the eye for it."

"You're right, I ain't," said Drum. "I got to hand it to you."

Drum got along well with David, better than other people did. He liked riding on the tail of all that energy, letting someone else do the organizing, listening to the rapid, precise flow of talk which he thought came from

David's having spent half a semester at Campbell College. But it was only words that should be so precise, not drums. David's drums never skipped a beat, and yet somehow the spirit was missing. Other drummers went into frenzies; David remained tight, expressionless, speeding faster and faster without so much as bending forward. "You drag," said Drum. "Oh, I feel it."

"I don't drag. I'm there all the way."

"Well, but you're holding me back somehow. Tying me in. *I* don't now."

"Get another drummer, if you feel like that."

But he never did. Together they went over each new piece, juggling lines and bickering and giving little wheezes of disgust at each other. When it came to music, Drum always won. He had the feel for it. "What's this talking out in the middle of a piece?" David once asked. "Where does that get you? Most of what you say is not even connected."

"I ain't going to argue about that," said Drum. "I just do it. If you have to ask why, you shouldn't be here."

"Oh, all right. I don't care."

He had the sense not to go against Drum on things like that. He believed that Drum was a real musician, someone who deserved to climb straight to the top. When an audience talked instead of listening, David muttered curses at them all the while he played. When Drum hit one of his low moods, David followed him around rescuing scraps of songs from wastebaskets. "What call have you got to slump around like this? What you throw away those other cats would give their teeth to write. You're nearly there. You've almost made it."

"You reckon so? I don't know. Maybe you're right," Drum would say finally.

David paid a visit to Evie Decker on a Saturday afternoon during finals. She was on her front porch studying. She lay in a wooden swing with her head on a flattened, flowered cushion, one foot trailing to the floor to keep her rocking. When she heard the Jeep, she turned and blinked. Swirls of color chased around its body and across the canvas top, where they blurred and softened. And there came Drum Casey's drummer out of the little tacked-on door, smoothing down his bangs with his fingers. "The Missouri Compromise," Evie went on out loud, "was supposed to maintain a . . ." but her eyes were on David. She watched him cross her yard and climb her steps, rifle-straight and full of purpose. Because of the edgeless shimmer of his hair in the sunlight, he seemed only another daydream, nothing to get nervous about. "Afternoon," he said.

"Afternoon," said Evie. She sat up, laying a finger in her history book to mark the place.

"You Evie Decker?"

But he would have known, having seen her forehead by now. She didn't answer.

"I'm David Elliott. I play with Drum Casey."

"I know, I recognized you," said Evie. She waited for him to go on, but he seemed to be getting his bearings. He gazed at the dim white house, at the lawn twinkling beneath a sprinkler, and finally at Evie herself, who wore a billowing muu-muu and no shoes. Then he said, "Mind if I talk with you a moment?"

"All right."

He sat on the top porch step, with his forearms resting on his knees. Now that he was in the shade he had lost his shimmer. He was made of solid flesh, damp from the heat. Evie began swinging back and forth very rapidly.

"I'm also his manager," said David.

"Yes, I know."

"I do his publicity, line up parties and things. I think we got a good sound going." He flashed her a look. "*Drum* has."

Evie stopped swinging.

"Drum has really got it," he told her. Why was he watching her feet? She curled her toes under. "Don't you think so?" he asked.

"Well, yes," said Evie. "You know I do." She brushed a loose piece of hair off her forehead. David peered at the scars and then lowered his eyes—something that usually made her angry. "What was it that you wanted to talk about?" she asked him.

"Oh. Well, you spoke to Drum the other day about a plan you had. Plan for publicity."

"Tuesday," said Evie.

"Was that right, you had a plan?"

"I thought if I went to his shows, and sat up front. *You* know. People would say, 'This boy has got to be good, look at what she did because of him.' Only your friend said—"

"It's not a bad idea," said David.

"Your friend said no."

"Ah, *he* don't know. That's why he has me."

"He said he couldn't sing under those conditions."

"What does he know?"

"He knows if he can sing or not," Evie said.

"Look. Do you want to try it? Just once, just tonight. If people take notice, you can stay. If not, you go. All right?"

"What, try just sitting there?"

"That's right. Tonight. I'll give you a lift, pick you up at eight. Three dollars and beer. Only don't drink a lot, you hear? It wouldn't look good."

"I never have but one beer anyway."

"Though on second thought, nothing wrong if you *did* drink a lot. It wouldn't hurt anything."

"I never have but one," Evie said.

"Oh, well."

He stood up and Evie stood with him, clutching her book. "Wait," she said.

"What is it?"

"Well, I don't know. I haven't thought it out yet, really—"

He paused, not arguing, just waiting. "About your friend," she said. "Drum, I mean. Well, I hate to go against him this way. Riding right over what he said to me. What will he do? Did he say anything about you coming here?"

"He didn't know about it," David said.

"Oh," said Evie.

"He leaves this kind of thing to me," David told her. He looked up suddenly, straight into her eyes. "You can't ever listen to *him*. Then where would he be? Playing in a room to himself, wasting all that music alone. I hate to see things wasted."

It seemed more settled then. Evie nodded and let him go.

At eight o'clock that night Evie came down the front steps in a skirt and blouse, her vinyl sandals, and a blue plastic headband that kept her hair off her face. The Jeep was already parked outside. In the back seat, behind David, Drum Casey sprawled out with both feet up and his guitar in the crook of his arm. It hadn't occurred to Evie that he might be there. She froze on the sidewalk, gripping her purse. Then David said, "Nope. It's not what I was thinking of."

"What?" she said.

"You need something black. Dressy."

"No one dresses up at the Unicorn."

"*You* do. You want to stand out. We'll wait."

"What? You want me to change *now*? I can't do that, my father will start wondering. He thinks I'm at a friend's."

"We'll wait around the block then."

"Oh, for Christ's sake," said Drum. David shooed him away with one hand.

"You leave this to me," he said. "I've got it all clear in my mind. We'll be over there, Evie."

Evie ran back to her room. She changed in a rush, mislaying things that had been right at her fingertips and tearing stockings, jamming zippers, tripping over cast-off clothing. If she took one minute too long, she felt, the Jeep would vanish. It would drift off like a tiny, weightless boat, piloted by careless people with short memories. She put on a scoop-necked black blouse and a black skirt. Then she picked up a pair of pumps and ran down the stairs in stocking feet. "Back in a while, Daddy," she called. Her father didn't answer. He might not even have heard.

The Jeep waited around the corner. Drum was plucking one guitar string over and over. He didn't stop when she climbed into the front seat, but David looked her over carefully and said, "That's right. Much better."

"Is this what I should wear all the time?"

"All the *time*?" said Drum. "How often you figure on doing this?"

Evie looked at David, who was backing the car up. He didn't answer. Finally she turned toward the back seat, and without actually meeting Drum's eyes she said, "If it works out, I'm coming every week."

"Ah, David," Drum said. "You've went too far this time."

"Will you leave it to me?" said David.

"You've went too far, man."

They drove the rest of the way without speaking. David frowned at the road, making some sort of calculations, shaking his head from time to time and then brightening as if an idea had struck. In the back, Drum kept plucking at the guitar string. Whenever the Jeep slowed, Evie could hear the single note repeating itself tinnily in the twilight.

They pulled in beside a motorcycle in the Unicorn's parking lot. Not many other cars had arrived yet. After he had shut the motor off, David said, "Now, listen. You'll sit at a table for one, right up front. I've brought you a candle. It'll stand out. While the other guy's on, Joseph Ballew, read a newspaper."

"By candle?"

"Oh, shoot now," Drum said. "Joseph Ballew is a friend of mine. She can't do that."

"Oh, all right. Stare down at your beer, then. What I want is a difference, you follow me? A difference that people will notice when Drum comes on. Sit up. Look close. I was thinking of some other things, but there hasn't been time to work them out. Sending him flowers, for instance."

"I would send them back," said Drum.

"I figured you would."

"Another thing," said Drum. "I want you both to listen good, now. I am not for any part of this plan. I don't approve, I never will approve. It makes me sick. And on top of that it won't work, because while I am playing, my entire audience will be whispering and pointing at a fat girl with a name on her forehead. I just thought you should know that."

Evie said, "Oh, well, I don't want to—"

"Got you," David told Drum. "Then I had thought

of having her scream, maybe, but I guess not. She's not the type for it.''

He looked at Evie for a minute longer, and then shook his head and climbed out of the Jeep. Evie had to trail behind them all the way across the parking lot.

The policeman at the door recognized her. He nodded at her and then rested his hands awkwardly on his gunbelt and stared into the distance. The proprietor recognized her too. When she walked in, he stepped out from behind the bar, smoothing his apron and looking worried. ''You're the girl that, uh. Look, I hope you're not planning to pull something like that again. I had an awful time. Cops were down my neck all night, thinking there had been a cutting.''

''There had been,'' David said.

''Not *that* kind.''

''Well, never mind. She's here to watch Drum sing, that's all. Have you got a table for one?''

''You know I ain't. People like sitting in groups.''

''Give me a bar stool then, we'll use that.''

He dragged the stool up next to the dance platform, and set a chair beside. It was the right height for a table but much too small, which David said was all for the better. ''Ruin everything if someone came and sat with you,'' he said. From a brown paper bag he took a tablecloth and a netcovered vase with a candle in it, the kind used in restaurants. Meanwhile Evie stood by awkwardly with her hands across her purse. Drum had disappeared somewhere. From a door behind the dance platform she heard laughter and the twanging of guitars.

''Sit down,'' said David.

She sat.

''No, not like that, Straighter. And don't put your purse on the table. I want you half-turned from the audience, not quite sideways, so that they can get a glimpse of—''

"I know how," Evie said. "Leave it to me. I can figure it out for myself."

And she did. She sat erect, her hands folded in her lap, an untouched beer in front of her. The candle glimmered more brightly on her face as the room grew darker. People filing in called out greetings to the proprietor, joked with their dates and scraped paths for themselves between the chairs, but when they saw the candle their voices seemed to skip a beat. They glanced at the candle and then at Evie. Evie stared straight ahead at nothing at all.

Drum Casey was the first to play that night. When he came onto the platform Evie looked up; nothing more. David signaled to her silently all through the first piece: "Do something. Move around. Could you stand? Take a drink." Evie ignored him. *"My girl has done and boarded a Carolina Trailways,"* Drum sang, *"She's scared to death of planes and she can't stand railways,"* and Evie stared at his face without blinking. Out of all the chattering couples dancing or at least beating time, Evie was the only one motionless. She showed them the white mound of her back disappearing into a scoop of black cotton, the curve of one cheek turned rigidly away. Her dowdy clothes gave her a matronly look; her scars, what could be seen of them, seemed in the candlelight to be mainly vertical, a new kind of age-line or tear track which made her appear experienced and incapable of being surprised. "See that girl?" someone whispered. "I believe it's the one in the newspaper. No, wait till she turns. Remember when I showed you her picture?" They were careful not to point. Girls indicated her by no more than a glance. "That's her. No, don't look now." In the back of the room, a boy half stood to peer at her before Fay-Jean Lindsay pulled him sharply down.

"*Will you see me to the door?*" Casey asked.

"*Don't come no further.*

"*Don't mind the lights.*

"*When you going to leave off that hammering?*

"*When they going to let me be?*"

Evie looked down at the table. David had stopped signaling to her by now. His eyes skimmed the roomful of people, who stared from Evie to Drum as if following a dotted line. Then he nodded to himself and turned all his attention to the song.

7

She was hired for life, David said, meaning for as long as she could cause any kind of stir, make a ripple cross a room and bounce off the wall to cross back. But how long would that be? She had felt, the first night, a buzz and a whispering at the back of her neck. On the following Saturday it was quieter. "Maybe I shouldn't be riding with you," she told David, although she would have fought against giving the rides up. "Won't it look funny? You and Drum bringing me here just to sit admiring you?"

"*They* don't care," said David. "It's like watching a magician. They would like to believe his cards really come from thin air."

David had other plans in mind. Now that Evie's had worked he had grown jittery, impatient to improve on it. He was nervous about the sheer understatement of a single dumpy girl sitting there with a beer. Shouldn't she drink too much? Cry? Send notes? But Evie said no. She walked a narrow line; it was all right to take money for lifting a scarred face toward a rock player every Saturday night but only if what she did was real, without a single piece of playacting. Her sitting still was real, and so was pinning her eyes on Drum. So were her scars, which turned white in time, raised and shiny, gleaming clean even if the rest of her face became

74

smudged in the heat. "How about a new costume?" David asked. "Blacker and shinier. With a rhinestone necklace." "No," said Evie. It was as clear a no as Drum's when he refused to stop his speaking out. David never brought the subject up again.

She offered to come to the Unicorn free. It wasn't as if she needed the money. David said, "Fine," but Drum, when he heard about it, said, "What is she trying to do to me? She gets paid. Then she can burn it, for all I care. But she gets paid, anyhow."

"Sometimes I feel like I am dealing with porcupines," David said.

School had ended. Evie spent the last few weeks of it feeling blurred and out of focus, with classmates looking carefully to the right and left of her and speaking to the middle button on her blouse. Even Fay-Jean Lindsay seemed to have trouble finding things to say to her. On the final day, they autographed annuals out on the school lawn. They had overlooked Evie other years—reaching across her to pass their annuals to someone else, sending her home with only a few scattered signatures in her own. But this year, everyone wanted her autograph. They shoved their books at her silently, with lowered eyes. "Best wishes, Evie Decker," she wrote. She felt awkward about trying the clever rhymes that other people used. Then, after signing for the twentieth or thirtieth time, she began marking the forehead of her photograph with Y ϶Ϥ϶ and nothing more. When the bell rang, she cleared out her locker and left the building without a backward glance.

"What do you do with yourself these days?" her father asked.

"Nothing much."

"Are you bored? Have you got a lot of time on your hands?"

"Oh, no."

Time hung in huge, blank sheets, split by Saturday nights. She spent her days bickering with Clotelia or carrying on listless, circular conversations with Violet. In the evenings she sat at her window slapping mosquitoes, gazing into darkness so heavy and still that it seemed something was about to happen, but nothing ever did. She awoke in the mornings feeling faded, with clammy bedclothes twisted around her legs.

On Saturday nights she took hours to dress. Her hair would be limp from constant re-arranging, her black skirt and blouse shiny at the seams from too much ironing. She held up and threw down endless pieces of costume jewelry. She brushed her black suede pumps until little rubber spots appeared. "Oh," her father would say, meeting her on the stairs. "Are you going out?"

"Just to Violet's."

"Have a nice time."

Why hadn't anyone told him where she went? He continued up the stairs, pulling keys and loose change and postage stamps from his pockets and stepping over the turned-up place in the carpet without even seeming to notice it.

She waited on the corner for the Jeep. Her arms were folded across her chest, as if, in this heat, she were cold. Sometimes her teeth chattered. What held her mind was not the time spent in the Unicorn but the rides there and back, the two half-hour periods in the Jeep. She thought of them as a gift. Someone might have said, "Do you want Drum Casey? Here is a half hour. Here is another. See what you can do." For while she was at the Unicorn, she never exchanged a word with Drum. He was either performing or off in the back room. Bearing that in mind, she talked non-stop all the way over and all the way back. She went against her own nature, even. She shoved down all her reserve and from her place in the front seat she drilled him with words.

"Can you read music? Do you believe in drugs? What was it got you started playing?"

"Course I read music, what do you think I am," said Drum, following a passing car with his eyes. "Marijuana gives me headaches. I won a talent show, that's how I started."

Oh, questions were the only way to grab his attention. She had tried, at first, declarative sentences: laying her life before him neatly and in chronological order, setting out minute facts about herself as if it were important he should know. Drum seemed not to hear. But she had only to say, "Is *all* your family musical?" for him to wade up from his silence and start framing an answer. "None of them's musical, they just admire it a whole lot. My mama said she would give every cent she had into seeing me be a singer."

"Doesn't she come to hear you play?"

"At the rock show she did. All my family did."

"Did I see them? What do they look like?"

"Nothing extra. Just a parcel of brothers and her and him."

"Him? Oh, your father. What does your father do?"

"What have you got up there," Drum said, "a questionnaire?" David, taking him literally for a second, glanced sideways into Evie's lap. But then Drum said, "He works in a filling station. I help him out some."

"I bet he's proud of you. Isn't he?"

"Oh, well."

"He would have to be," said Evie. "Anybody that plays like you, his family must just *die* of pride."

His eyes would flick over to her, as sudden and as startling as the appearance of someone in a vacant window. If she spoke about his music he would listen all day, but what would he answer?

"Oh, well, I don't know."

She entered the Unicorn alone and went to her table, keeping her head erect, holding her stomach in. Eyes lit on her back. Whispers flitted across tables. "Oh, it's you," the proprietor said. "Budweiser?"

"Yes, please, Zack. Have you got a match for my candle?"

She thought of herself as a bait-and-switch ad. People came out of curiosity, bored by the long summer days. They figured they might as well go stare at the girl who had ruined her face. But after two minutes of that, there was nothing left to do but concentrate on the singer who had caused it all. Even Drum had to see that. People who returned came for the music alone; Evie was only a fixed character to be pointed out knowingly to new customers. *"Will you be waiting?"* Drum called. "Where *will you be waiting*?" Customers who were used to his speaking out began answering. "Yeah, man! Here!" A reviewer commented on him in the *Avalice and Farinia Weekly.* "Rock music of his own making, leaning toward a country sound, original at first although he tends to get repetitious." Evie was not mentioned, any more than the color of his clothes or the brand of his guitar.

Evie always had to hang around for awhile before the ride back. The wait was nerve-wracking. It sometimes stretched on till after one o'clock in the morning, while at home her father might be telephoning Violet at any moment. She watched the customers gather their belongings and leave. The proprietor washed his glass mugs. The dance platform was dark and empty, and all she heard of Drum was fits of music in the back room. "David," she would say, catching his sleeve as he hurried by, "are we going now? What's taking so long?"

"Be just a moment," David always said. But he would be carrying in a new pitcher of beer and a fistful of mugs. Eventually Evie gave up. She tucked her purse under her arm and left, sidling between vacant chairs and crossing the dim-lit, hollow-sounding floor to the door. Outside, the darkness would be cool and transparent. She took several deep breaths before she curled up in the back seat of the Jeep.

The slick surface of Drum's guitar would jog her awake. "Move over," he would say. "Here we are."

"What time is it?"

"I don't know."

Until she looked at her watch she always had a lost, sinking feeling. Her sleep had been troubled and filled with muddled dreams; it might have lasted for minutes or for hours. Had her father called the police yet? She pressed forward in her seat, as if that would help them get home faster. Every pickup truck dawdling in front of them made her angry. Then she remembered Drum. On the rides home he sat beside her, with only the guitar between them. "Did you think it went well?" she asked him.

"Mmm."

"They liked the Carolina Trailways song."

No answer. David took over for him. "I thought so too. Why always that one? The walking song is a hell of a lot harder to do."

He was kind-hearted, David was. Or maybe he just wanted to keep Evie's good will. During Drum's silences he picked up the tail of the conversation and moved smoothly on with it, rescuing her. For a while they would shoot sentences back and forth—"Oh, well, the walking song takes getting used to." "Not if they had *ears* it wouldn't"—but there was always the consciousness of Drum's silence, which they played to like actors on a stage. Questions, that was the only way. Questions.

"What is your favorite song, Drum? Drum?"

"Oh, I don't know."

"Don't you have a favorite?"

"Not for all time I don't. The one about the blue jeans, maybe."

"Why don't you have regular titles?"

"Never had no need for them."

"You will when you make a record," Evie said.

His eyes flicked over to her again; she felt them in the dark. She moved his guitar slightly so as to speak straight at him. "Someone is going to make a record of you that will sell a million copies," she told him. "What will they put on that little center label? You've got to think up some titles."

"She's right," David said.

"What's so hard about that?" said Drum. "I'll name them what I call them—'The Walking Song.' 'The Blue Jeans Song,' nothing to it. Wait till they ask me, first."

"You think they won't ask you?"

"They haven't yet, have they? I been sitting in that dump for seven months now. Haven't got nowhere."

"You will," Evie said.

"How? When? You seen any talent scouts around?"

After a show he was always like that. She had seen girls clustering around him three deep at the end of a set, paying him compliments and brushing bits of nothing off his shoulder while Evie frowned fiercely into her beer and thought, "Now he'll find out; they'll show him he's too good for Pulqua and the Unicorn and me"—although she had always counted on his becoming famous. But when the girls left he would only seem more uncertain. His proud cold envelope of air temporarily left him. "You sound better than *anyone* I hear on the radio," Evie would tell him, and he would stun her by turning on her suddenly and saying, "You think so? Is that what you think? Ah, but what do *you* know?"

"I know if it sounds good."

"*I* don't know that. How do you know?"

Those were the only times they met face to face. They were the only times Evie lost the feeling that she was tugging at Drum's sleeve while he stood with his back to her, gazing outwards toward something she couldn't see.

Early in July, the Unicorn began hiring Drum for Fridays as well. People were asking for him, the proprietor said. Joseph Ballew was no longer enough. But Fridays Drum worked late in the A & P, bagging groceries. "The only solution," said David, sitting in the Jeep with one of his lists on the steering wheel, "is for me to pick you up first, Evie. Then we'll get Drum at the very last minute. Even then it'll be close. Does that suit you?"

"Of course," Evie said.

"Or you could keep coming just on Saturdays, if you wanted."

"Why? Do you think I'm not working out any more?"

"No, Lord, you're working out fine. But if your father starts worrying, you being gone two evenings and all—"

"No, I'll come," Evie said. Although it did seem that her father might begin to wonder. She frowned down at her skirt, gathering it in folds between her knees, while David made more lists on more scraps of paper.

The next Friday they drove to Farinia to pick up Drum. Evie had been through Farinia often, but without really noticing. She stared out her window now at the town's one paved street, with its double row of unpainted stores covered in rusty soft-drink signs. On a corner next to a shoe repair shop, a service station sat under a tent of flapping pennants, its lights already shining. David drove in and honked his horn.

"You haven't run over the bell thing yet," Evie told him.

"Bell thing? Oh. No, I don't want gas, this is where Drum lives."

"Here?"

Then she saw that the service station was an unpainted Victorian house, its bottom story tiled with shiny white squares. Above, lace curtains wavered in narrow windows. "What the hell," David said. "I'll run up and get him."

"Can I come too?"

"If you want."

She followed him across the service area and up a flight of rickety outside steps. The door had a card thumbtacked to it saying "ObeD E. CAseY" in pencil. David knocked. "Who is it?" a woman called.

"It's me, David. I've come for Bertram, tell him."

The door opened. After the rickety steps and the penciled card, Drum's mother was a relief—a plump, cheerful woman in a bibbed apron, smile lines working outward from Drum's brown eyes. "Evening, David," she said. Then she saw Evie, and she raised her fingers to her lips. "Oh, my Lord," she said. "Why, you must be—my Lord. Come in, honey. I hate to say it but I've forgotten what they called you."

"This is Evie Decker, Mrs. Casey," David said.

The name on Evie's face, of course, was Mrs. Casey's own—something Evie hadn't thought of before. But Mrs. Casey didn't seem to mind. She only looked worried; she shepherded Evie to a chair and hovered over her while Evie sat down. "Here, honey, put a cushion at your back. It's much more comfortable. My!" she said, staring openly at Evie's forehead. "I never thought it would be so, so *large*!"

David, still beside the door, shifted his weight uneasily. "Where is Bertram?" he asked. "We're running late."

"Oh, he's just now changing. I'll hurry him along."

She disappeared, looking backward one last time, and David sank down in a flowered armchair. The room was dim but clean, with a line of vinyl plants on the window sill and stiff plastic antimacassars on every piece of furniture. Over the mantel was a picture of a cross with a radiant gilt sunset just behind it. The glass-faced bookcase contained three books and dozens of photographs in white paper folders, which Evie rose to look at more closely. Towheaded boys scowled out at her, three or four to a picture. One was Drum, his hair turning darker and longer as he grew. In the most recent picture he was posed all alone with his guitar held vertically on one knee. "Would you believe that he was ever blond?" Mrs. Casey said behind her. "Then one day it seemed it all turned black, surprised the life out of me. The others, now, they're turning too. Bertram's daddy says his did the same."

"It's a good picture of him," Evie said.

"Would you like it?"

"Oh, no, I—"

"Go on, take it, we have more. It's the least I can do. Honey, I feel I *owe* you something. 'Bertram,' I said (I never call him Drum), 'that little girl has put your name in the paper and started you on your way. Now don't you forget that,' I said, and sure enough, here they are having him work Fridays too and I just know you had a part in it. Oh, how can you sit up at your little table that way? I heard all about it. 'She is doing you just a magnificent service, Bertram,' I said—"

"I'm sure they'd have started him on Fridays anyway," Evie told her. "He's the best singer I know of."

"Now aren't you sweet? Well, I can't say it myself, of course, being his mother, but deep down I know he has a wonderful career in front of him. He is what I am pinning my hopes on. 'You remember,' I tell him, 'that wherever you go, you are carrying my hopes around with you.' And it's on account of me that he's not just a filling-station attendant like his daddy. 'Boy's lazy,' his daddy says. 'Nineteen years old,' he says, 'and spinning out his days plucking music, only pumping gas when it suits him.' I tell him I won't stand for that kind of talk. 'You just remember,' I tell him, 'that Bertram is going to be famous one day. He's carrying all my hopes,' I say. There's a spark in Bertram, you know? He gets it from my side. My father played the banjo. Not just being musical but a sort of, *I* don't know—"

Evie nodded, over and over. Agreement welled up inside her like tears, but even saying yes meant breaking into Mrs. Casey's web of words. "There was always something special about him," said Mrs. Casey. "Right from when he was born. I felt it. Would you like to see the album?"

"We got to go, Mom," Drum said. He was standing in the living room doorway, buckling his belt. "Don't wait up for me."

"Oh, why do you rush off like this? Bertram, honey, I want you to bring Evie back again, you hear? We just get along like a house afire. I hope you will never be so famous you forget the people who did you a good turn."

"A good turn, what's she been telling you? I'm paying her, ain't I?"

"Not to do all that cutting you didn't. Can't *any* money pay for that. Evie, honey, what do the doctors say?"

"I don't know," said Evie.

"Well, you might just inquire. When Bertram leaves this area I expect they could fix you up just like new."

"Mom, for Lord's sake," Drum said.

"Well, she don't want it all her life, now does she?"

"We better be going," David said. He stood up and ran his fingers through his hair. "Nice seeing you, Mrs. Casey."

"Well, hurry back." And at the door, as she handed Evie the picture in its paper folder, she said, "Don't be a stranger, Evie, we'll welcome you just as often as you want to come. Next visit I'll let you see Bertram in the photo album, you hear?"

"Thank you," said Evie. She was surprised to feel David's hand suddenly clasp her elbow as she started down the steps.

She went back often. Drum usually had to be called for on Fridays, and it was Evie who ran up to knock on the door while David waited in the Jeep. "I don't see how you stand that woman," he said.

"Why? I think she's sweet."

"How can you listen to all that talk? And going on about your forehead and all, how can you put up with that?"

"Oh, I don't mind," said Evie.

She thought that David might even like her now, in an absent-minded way. They had had so many long rides together, with the filling of the silence resting on the two of them—Drum being absent or as good as absent, twanging that one guitar string. Once when they were alone David said, "I've been thinking about your forehead. I mean, they're only white now, the letters. Have you ever thought of wearing bangs?"

"Then no one in the Unicorn would see them," Evie said.

"Well, no."

"Don't you want me to come to the Unicorn any more?"

"No, I was thinking about the rest of the time. People must stare at you a lot. Your friends and them."

"I don't have any friends," said Evie.

"Oh."

"Only Violet, and she doesn't stare. And besides, by now I don't notice. I don't even see the letters in the mirror, half the time. Sometimes I wonder: Does *anybody* see them? Or have I just gotten adjusted? Do they come as a shock to strangers still?"

"They do stand out some," David said.

"A lot?"

"Well, I don't know—"

"You can tell me, I don't care. Are they bad?"

"Well, not with bangs they wouldn't be."

"I see," said Evie.

But she still didn't get around to cutting bangs.

At the end of July a heat wave struck. Crops shriveled, lawn sprinklers ran all day and all night, Clotelia carried a black umbrella to fend off the sun and Violet stopped wearing underwear. "Seems like this summer will just go on forever," people said. But Evie thought of the heat wave as the peak of the season, a dividing point after which summer would slide rapidly downhill toward fall. And how could she go back to school? She had never planned past August. She had cleaned out her locker with the feeling that she was leaving for good, and the thought of going back to the rigid life of winter smothered her.

Lately her rapid-fire questions to Drum had slackened off, grown easygoing. "I suppose you'll be playing at a party tomorrow," she would say, too hot and lazy even to add a question mark. All Drum had to answer was, "Mmm" and lapse into silence again. But the thought of summer's ending came to her one Friday night at the Unicorn. Drum was speaking out: *"Was it you I heard crying?"* "Yes!" someone shouted. But Evie hadn't been listening. She didn't even know what song he was on. Then she was riding home in the Jeep, picking absently at a seam in his guitar. Drum jerked it away from her. His face was turned to the window, only the smooth line of one cheek showing. What had happened to all her spring plans? Things were no different from the very first night.

She changed her tempo. She concentrated on Drum alone, running a race with time, which she pictured as a hot, dark wind. "Why do you speak out in songs? Oh, you're going to say you don't know, but you could tell me what started it. Was it by accident? Did you just want to give a friend a message or something?"

"I forget," Drum said.

"Think. When was the first time you did it?"

"Oh, well, the picnic song, I reckon. That's right. It was too short. I tossed in extra lines, speaking out, like, just the pictures in my mind. Then a girl told me it was a good gimmick."

"What girl? Do I know her?"

"That's none of your business."

"Nothing you speak out is connected," Evie said. "How can so many pictures come to your mind at once?"

"I don't know."

She noticed that people in the Unicorn had stopped staring at her. No one whispered about her; no one stood up to get a better look. They craned their necks around her in order to see the musicians. Sooner or later David would notice too. She dreaded his firing her. As if she could change anything by beating him to the draw, she came right out with the news herself one evening when they were alone. "People are not whispering when I walk in nowadays," she told him.

"I saw."

"Does that mean I should stop coming?"

"Well, let me see what Drum says."

She knew what Drum would say.

Then next Friday night when David picked her up, she told him the entire plot of a movie without giving him time for a single word. When the plot was finished she analyzed it, and when that was finished she told him Clotelia's life story. By then they had picked up Drum and arrived at the Unicorn. Neither Drum nor David had had a chance to say she was fired. It will be afterwards, she thought, when we are riding home. All during the show she sat memorizing the cold smell of beer, the texture of her netted candle-vase and the sight of Drum Casey tossing his hair above her as he sang. After that night it would all be lost, a summer wasted.

But on the ride home they had other things to talk about. "You hear the news?" Drum asked her. Evie only stared. Drum never began conversations.

"We're going to a night club in Tar City. A man came looking for me, all the way to the Unicorn, hired me for a two-week run. I thought it would *never* happen."

"This is the beginning, now," David said. "Didn't I tell you? A genuine night club where they serve set-ups. From here on out we'll be heading straight up."

"But what about the Unicorn?" Evie asked.

"Oh, we'll take two weeks off. It's all set."

"And may not be back," said Drum. "I tell you, after this I'm going to buy me some new singing clothes. Spangly."

"Well, congratulations," said Evie, but no one heard

her. They were discussing lights and money and transportation.

When they reached Farinia, Drum said, "Let's wake Mom and tell her the news. Tell her we want a celebration." He might have been speaking only to David; Evie wasn't sure. The two of them bounded across the darkened service area while Evie followed at a distance, hanging back a little and looking around her and stopping to search in her pocketbook for nothing at all.

Mrs. Casey wore a pink chenille bathrobe, and her hair was set in spindly metal curlers all over her head. When she opened the door her hand flew to the curlers. "Bertram, my land, I thought you was alone," she said.

"Now, Mom, did you wait up again?" Drum circled her with one arm, nearly pulling her off her feet. "Listen, Mom. We want us a celebration. A man came and hired us to play two weeks at the Parisian."

"Is that right? Well, now," she said. When she was pleased her cheeks grew round and shiny, and little tucks appeared at the corners of her mouth. "I was just mixing up hot chocolate. Will you all have some?"

"Nah. Beer."

She talked even while she was out in the kitchen, freezing the three of them into silence. They sat in a row on the couch and looked toward the doorway. "I just know this is the break you been waiting for," she called. "Once you're in the city your name gets around more. Oh, I've half a mind to wake your daddy. Won't *he* be surprised. 'Now,' I'll say, 'tell me again who's wasting time when he should be pumping gas?' The Parisian is a right famous place, you know. A lot of important people go there. Remember your cousin Emma, Drum? That's where she had the rehearsal supper, before her wedding. I was there. Well, little did I *dream*, of course, at the time. Is Evie going too?"

Evie stared at the doorway until it blurred.

"What for?" Drum asked.

"Why, to sit at her little table."

"Nah," said Drum.

"Oh, go on, Evie."

David cleared his throat. "As a matter of fact, Evie's been thinking of quitting," he said. "Weren't you, Evie?"

"That's right."

"She feels the point has been made, by now. No sense going on with it."

"Well, no, I suppose not," said Mrs. Casey.

She appeared in the doorway with three cans of beer on a pizza tin. "She might want to come with your daddy and me and just *watch*, though," she said.

"She don't," said Drum.

"Will you let her speak for herself?"

Everybody looked at Evie. Evie stared down at her laced fingers and said, "I don't know. If it was up to *me*, I mean—I might want to come just once and hear him play."

"There now. You see?" Mrs. Casey told Drum.

Drum slammed his beer down on the coffee table. "Will you get her off my *back*?" he said.

"Bertram!"

"Now, I mean this. I have had it. How do you think it feels to look at that face night after night when I'm playing? Do you think I like it? Following me with those eyes, watching every move. It wasn't *my* fault she cut those fool letters. Am I going to have to go on paying for it forever?"

"Bertram. No one's asking you to pay for it. She just wants to come hear your music, that's all."

"Don't make me laugh," said Drum.

"Oh, you're turning hard, son. Are you going to be one of those stars that forgets the little people?"

"Well, wait now," said David. He stood up. "Seems to me we're getting worked up over nothing. If Drum don't want Evie in the audience she won't come. Right, Evie?"

"Right," said Evie. The word opened a door, letting through a flashing beam of anger that took her by surprise. "I won't come now or *ever*. Ever again. Not if that's the way he feels."

"Praise the Lord," said Drum.

"And another thing, Drum Casey. If I had known what a cold and self-centered person you are those letters wouldn't be there, I can promise you that. And your music is boring, it tends to get repetitious, and I hope everybody at the Parisian notices that the very first night and sends you home again. I hope you cry every mile of the way."

"Why, Evie," Mrs. Casey said.

"Not only that, but you can't even play the guitar. You just hammer out noise like any fool at a Coke party, and I hope they notice that too."

"That's a lie," said Drum. "You're talking crazy."

"Oh, am I?" She stood, but her knees felt shaky and she sat down again. "I may not be musical but I know *that* much. Joseph Ballew can play better any day."

"He can not. Joseph don't know one end of the guitar from the other."

"That's more than you know."

"You're out of your head. I play a great guitar. Don't I, David?"

"Why, surely you do," Mrs. Casey said.

"All you've got going," said Evie, "is the speaking out and me. Well, the speaking out does not make sense and I'm going to cut my hair in bangs. *Then* see how far you go."

"I was working at the Unicorn before I ever heard your name. I didn't notice anyone asking how come no girl had cut 'Casey' in her forehead. Did you, David?"

"It was a waste," Evie said.

"Will you stop that talk?"

"It was all for nothing."

"I play a great guitar," Drum said.

On the way home, Evie cried into the hem of her skirt. David kept quiet. When they had reached her house he said, "That ties it, I guess."

"I'm sorry," Evie said.

"No harm done."

From what she could see in the dark, he seemed to be smiling. She smiled back and smoothed her skirt down. "Well, it looks like I won't be seeing you again," she said.

"No, I guess not. Been quite an experience knowing you, though."

"Well. Good-bye."

Before she shut the car door behind her she made certain she hadn't forgotten anything. She wanted to leave no traces, not even a scrap of paper fluttering on the floor to make them remember her and laugh. Her father was downstairs reading, wearing his faded plaid bathrobe. "I was just about to call Violet," he said. "Aren't you a little late?"

"We ran into some friends."

"Oh. There's cocoa in the kitchen."

"I don't want any."

She started toward her room, but halfway up the stairs she thought she heard his voice. "Did you say something?" she called.

"I said, are those the only clothes you've got? Remind me in the morning to give you some shopping money."

"I don't want any," Evie said.

8

She cut herself a set of bangs, long enough to cover her eyebrows. Her eyes without eyebrows looked worried and surprised. And because her hair was puffy at the sides, she sometimes had the feeling she was living under a mushroom button. "*There's* my girl," her father said. "I'm going to find you a plastic surgeon, too. Would you go? I always knew you would come out of this, if I just let you be." Then he went off to paint the back porch, whistling a tune she couldn't recognize.

She threw away her black skirt and blouse, her snapshot of Drum at the Unicorn, Fay-Jean's pencil drawing and the posed photograph his mother had given her. That was all that was left of him. She walked downtown under Clotelia's huge umbrella and laid in a stack of school supplies for the coming year. On the way home she bought a Tar City newspaper. "Like everything else," she read, "night-life seems to be suffering from the heat wave. The Manhattan Club has no entertainment at all this week, and the Parisian's Drumstrings Casey is strictly amateur." She refolded the newspaper and pushed it through the swinging door of a trashcan.

Afternoons, she visited Violet. All summer she had stayed home and let Violet come to her, and now she felt as if she had returned from some long hard trip that no one else knew about. The off-hand clutter of Violet's room and her smiling fat family had a clear and distant look. New china horses had joined the parade across Violet's bureau. On the closet door was a life-size poster of a movie star she had never even heard of. "What have you been doing all summer?" she asked Violet.

"What do you mean? You've seen me every day, haven't you?"

"Well, yes." She sat forward on the bed, cupping her chin in her hand. "Seems like I had *two* summers," she said. "Two different ones. Sometimes I think, was that *me*, riding large as life between two boys to a road-house? Why, I never was on a date, even, except with that peculiar Buddy Howland whose voice never changed. I can't believe I did it all."

"Oh, remembering things is always that way," Violet said.

"Not for me. Nothing to *bother* remembering, before. And I would rather not remember this. Why was I such a fool? You should have stopped me."

"The best thing now is just to drop the subject from your mind," Violet said.

"You're right. I will. Let's talk about something else. Did you know my father is taking over Miss Cone's class? He said that she—"

"You told me that."

"I did?"

"Last month."

"Oh. I forgot." She rose sharply from the bed, causing Violet to grab for her bottle of nail polish. "You see what I mean. I don't remember telling you a thing about it. Oh, how am I going to get over all this? I wish I had spent the summer swimming or being a camp counselor. Or just snug in my house reading books, even. I wish someone would give me back all the time

I've known Drum Casey, and I would change everything I did.''

"You were going to drop the subject," Violet said.

But she couldn't. She spent her mornings skating a slick surface, keeping busy, but afternoons she sprawled across Violet's unmade bed and said the same things again and again, and Violet listened with a sort of cheerful tolerance that made it seem safe to say them.

On Monday morning, over a week since her fight with Drum, Evie settled down to cleaning out her desk. It helped to do things with bustle in them. Just as she started on the second drawer she heard Clotelia call, "Evie? You wanted down here."

"Coming," said Evie. She came out and looked down the stair well to the front hall. Clotelia stood waiting there with her arms folded and her feet apart. "You got a guest," she said.

"Who is it?"

"Come on down, I told you."

"Oh, all right."

"Your father be home any minute, now."

"Well, what about it?"

But Clotelia only jerked a thumb toward the living room. Downstairs, Drum Casey was sitting on the couch with his boots on the coffee table. His head lolled to one side, as if he were asleep. Evie stopped short in the doorway and stared at him. She felt separated from him by a wall of glass, protected by the thick new bangs on her forehead and the days she had spent removing him from her mind in bits and crumbs. His eyes were closed; she could look at his face without feeling he might blind her by looking back. His mouth was relaxed, almost open. He needed a shave. His hands, with their nails cut short for the guitar strings, lay loosely curled on his legs. When she saw his hands she made a small movement, only enough to smooth her bangs down, but Drum rolled his head toward her and looked from beneath lowered lids. "Hey," he said.

"Hello," said Evie.

He sat up and moved his feet off the coffee table. The silence grew to the point where it would be hard to break. "I didn't know it was you," Evie said finally. "Clotelia didn't say. Do you want a lemonade? You're hot, I bet—"

Behind her, Clotelia said, "Your father be home any minute, Evie."

"Oh. Yes, my father's coming," Evie said.

But that didn't seem to mean anything to Drum. He sat forward and rubbed his eyes with the heels of his hands. "I ain't slept since Saturday," he said.

"What happened?"

"I got fired."

"*What?*"

"Fired, I said."

"Oh, well, they don't know," said Evie, thinking of the reviews. "It's the weather. In this heat they can't tell good music from bad."

"Music, hell. That was just an excuse. I was getting on good with the manager's daughter and he didn't like it, that's all. Said I hadn't worked out well. 'Goddam man that *hires* these people—' he said. I said, 'Nobody does that to *me*.' End of it all was a fight."

"A fight? With fists?"

"What else. Fists and the police station and the works. He was just peeved over his daughter is all."

Evie blinked, cutting off the daughter forever with a single movement. "That's illegal," she said. "You can hold him to his contract."

"*Contract*, what do you think I am? A movie star?"

"Well, he can't just fire you."

"Guess again." Drum took a comb from his shirt pocket. "Now they got my name on the books, down at the police station. Just what I needed. You ever seen those movies where the mother tells the cops, 'He's a good boy?' That's what *my* mother did. 'He's a good boy,' she says. Then she paid the damages and yanked me outdoors and said she might've known this would happen. Said I had disgraced them all, what would my daddy say, if she had had any sense she would have put me to work like everyone told her to. Now, I ask you. Won't my own *family* even stand by me? When I got home my daddy wouldn't let me in the house. 'I am just too pissed off to look at you right now,' he says. 'Sleep down in the car. I'll talk with you in the morning.' 'Well, if *that's* the way you feel,' I said, and walked right off. I don't care if I never see the place again."

"Where is David?" Evie asked.

"David. Home, I reckon. *He* didn't get in no fight, not him. I would've gone and spent the night at his house but you know his mother, she hates my guts."

"What for?"

"No reason *I* know of. I never did a thing to her."

Out in the hallway, Clotelia gave a sudden sharp sigh. "Go fix some lemonade," Evie told her.

"Evie, your father going to hit the roof if he find him here."

"Never mind, fix some lemonade."

Clotelia pivoted on one heel and left. Drum seemed not to have noticed her. He combed his hair, ran one hand across it, and put the comb back in his pocket. "I spent the night on someone's porch," he said, "but didn't sleep none. Now my eyelids feel scratchy. I don't know what my daddy has against me, but he never will listen to reason, not for one second. Never asks my side of nothing. Oh, well, him I'm used to. But Mom? 'Bertram, you have just killed my soul,' she told me. 'I ain't got no more faith in you.' Mom! What would you say to that? I went by home this morning after I saw his service truck pull out and, 'Mom,' I said, 'could I just have some biscuits and a little side meat for my breakfast?' She said, 'Yes, here, I done saved you some, but you better not come by no more, Bertram, until you set it right. Meaning make up the money and apologize and get you a steady job.' Well, I never thought I would live to hear *her* talk that way. 'Now you *know* it wunt my fault,' I told her. 'That man is just real possessive over his daughter and for no good reason either, since she is right wild and always has been. But he just won't see it,' I said, 'and up and fired me on some manufactured cause.' Mom says, 'Oh, Bertram, where are you going to end up? Sometimes I feel you won't even amount to a hill of beans,' she says, and then she pushed a little brown bag of food on me. Well, it was like I had just heard something crack, the final floorboard I was resting on. I won't be going back now.''

He stood and began walking around the edges of the room. Every now and then he took a hand from his back pocket to pick up a figurine or a photograph. ''Who's this?'' he asked.

''My mother.''

''She dead? Who's this?''

''My uncle.''

''You got a real nice place here. You reckon your father might let me sleep on the couch?''

''Well, no, I doubt it.''

''How about your porch?''

''Not there either, I'm sure of it.''

''He'd never know.''

"He might," said Evie. "If a neighbor saw you, or he went out on the porch some night."

"I'd be real careful."

"But I was just getting all *straight*," said Evie. "How can you ask me a thing like that?"

All Drum did was pick up a china goose girl and lay it against his cheek, as if it cooled him.

"Oh, go ahead, then," said Evie. "I don't care."

So he slept on the porch, on the heavy, flattened cushions in the wooden swing. Not just one night, but all week. Evie would lie awake until midnight or so, when she heard through her open window the rusty sound of boots on the floorboards and then the creaking of the swing as he settled himself. The creaking died away immediately, with nothing following. He seemed not even to turn in his sleep. He would be one of those people who lay down without a fuss and lost consciousness until morning, frustrating whoever was with them, the way Violet did when she spent the night. It was Evie who stayed awake. She listened to crickets and breaths of music and other people's parties, and she thought of a hundred different things that could happen if her father came upon Drum. Would he shout? Call the police? Or only apologize for disturbing Drum's sleep and tiptoe back to bed? She expected to have nightmares about it, but when she finally slept her dreams were of struggling in water as thick as gelatin, running from a fire on boneless legs, climbing a ladder which swooped backwards under her weight but never quite fell over. When she awoke in the mornings, Drum was always gone.

After the first night she came out on the porch in her bathrobe and stared at the swing, whose cushions were not even dented. She was still there when Clotelia came. "He gone?" Clotelia asked. No one had told her Drum was staying there, but she seemed to know anyway. Evie nodded.

"Well, go on get dressed. Nothing attractive about sitting out here in your bathrobe."

At ten o'clock, her father went off for an errand. As soon as his car was out of sight Drum opened the front screen door a few inches and slid into the hallway. "I wonder if I could have breakfast?" he said. Evie was at the foot of the stairs, sorting out the mail. It was the first time all morning that Drum had not been in the center of her mind, and she raised her head and stared at him a minute. Then Clotelia called, "Come on out, it's on the table." She had set a place, even—a dinner plate heaped with ham and biscuits, which Evie and her father never ate. When Drum walked in, Clotelia looked up from the sink to say, "It's waiting on you, over there. I know *you.*" Then she emptied the dishwater and walked out, peeling off pink rubber gloves. Drum shrugged and sat down.

"She is a mite uppity," he said.

"Did you sleep all right?"

"Sure. It's little short, but better than the ground. You got any syrup?"

Evie handed it to him and then sat down. "Have you been to see David yet?" she asked.

"Not yet."

"How about your friends?"

"How about them?"

"Well, you do have some."

"Sure."

"Are they worried about you?"

He frowned at her over a biscuit. "What you getting at?" he asked.

"I'm not getting at anything."

"You want me to clear out?"

"No, of course not."

"What you asking about friends for, then?"

"I just wanted to know—" said Evie. She drew rays out from a coffee ring, with Drum watching. "I was wondering why it was me you came to," she said finally.

"Oh. I don't know."

"There must have been lots of other people."

"Sure."

She gave up. She waited until he had finished eating, and then she brought him an ash tray. Drum tipped back in his chair to smoke a cigarette. At his elbow was the back door, unlocked and waiting in case her father should appear. There was no telling when he might walk in. She sat braced to move suddenly, her mind tracking down and identifying every sound from the street, so that when finally Drum decided to answer her question she didn't take it in. "You and me really had some fight that night," he said. Evie said, "Mmhmm." She was listening to a jingling noise that could have been her father's Volkswagen. When it passed she said, "What?"

"You and me really had some fight, I said."

"Oh, well."

Drum blew out a funnel of smoke and watched it dissolve. Then he said, "I thought about it later. That fight is where I went wrong, I thought."

"Oh, well, it's over now," Evie said.

"It came to me the night I got fired. I said, 'Oh, damn, I missed all the signs, will you look at that?' "

"What?"

"Are you listening to me?"

"I just don't see what you're saying," Evie said. "It's all right about the fight, really. I'm the one that should apologize."

"I ain't apologizing, I meant every word. You weigh

on my head. But you bring luck, too. Or take it away, like when you hoped I would mess up at the Parisian.''

"Well, wait—" Evie said.

"If I'd of took you to the Parisian like you asked, they wouldn't have fired me."

"That's just silly," Evie said.

"Nothing silly about it. Except I wish if you bring me luck you wouldn't have to weigh on my head. Don't you ever *smile* none?"

"Of course I do."

"Not to notice. Just sitting there paper-faced with your forehead showing. Now you've cut bangs."

"I thought it was time to."

"Does that mean you were serious?"

"Serious about *what*?" Evie said. "I don't understand what we're talking about."

"The fight. When you said I couldn't play the guitar."

"Oh, that."

"I can play one hell of a lot better than Joseph Ballew, I'll tell you that. And sing too. If you don't agree, you got no ears."

"Well, I was just angry," Evie said. "I never really meant it."

"Did you know I took lessons? Up at Farnham's Music Company, where I got my guitar. Then I won a talent show before I had even finished my lessons. Fifteen dollars and a medal."

"You know I never meant it," Evie said. "It was just one of those things you say when you're angry. I could listen all day when you play."

"Well, then," said Drum. It seemed to be what he had come for. He stubbed his cigarette out and then just sat there, tipping his chair against the wall, until they heard Evie's father climbing the porch steps. "See you around," Drum said. He was up from his chair and out of the house before Evie could answer. He must have taken note of that door right from the beginning.

When he was gone, she felt she had made a mistake. He had come to make sure she still liked his singing; if she had had any sense, she would have kept him wondering. She plodded from room to room pulling sharply on one strand of hair, muttering under her breath when she was sure she was alone. "Was I serious? I don't know. I've forgotten what you sound like by now." Clotelia passed her several times, and threw her a look but said nothing. Her father asked if she were bored. "No, why?" Evie said.

"I thought you looked restless."

"Oh, no."

"Well, school will start soon. Summer always drags about this time."

He looked so cheerful nowadays. He had made her an appointment with a plastic surgeon for September, and at supper he had grown talkative and sometimes made small jokes. What she should have said was, "No. I don't like you anymore, I don't like your music, I don't want you sleeping on my porch." Then life would be simple again. No more hanging around waiting and wondering, no more secrets hidden from her whistling, unsuspecting father.

Drum set up a pattern. He came whenever her father was gone, as if he kept close watch on the house, and he seldom spoke. Conversation was up to Evie. If she was silent he seemed irritable, tapped his fingers or swung his foot, left before he had to. If she talked he seemed not to listen, but kept very still. He rested the back of his head against the wall and watched the ceiling while she searched for any words at all to fill the space. "You mustn't mind Clotelia. Does she get on your nerves? Once I went home with her when my fa-

ther was out of town and I met her boyfriend, not the
one she has now but another one, who sat around drinking beer all the time and matching pennies, living off
her money. She thinks all men do that way. That's the
only reason she acts so snippy. His name was, wait a
minute. Not Spencer, no—"

She had never been given so much time before. No
one interrupted her, no one shifted impatiently. She
could choose her words as slowly as luxury items in a
department store. "Not Steward, not Stengle. It will
come to me in a moment. Spindle. I knew it was something peculiar. Have you ever heard of anyone named
Spindle? He had a black knitted skull cap on in the
middle of summer. His shoes were the big high kind
with metal toe-caps."

Drum stubbed his cigarette out and passed a hand
over his eyes. "Are you tired?" Evie asked him.

"No."

But his face was pinched and tight, and his tan was
turning yellow. Sometimes, lost in what she was saying,
she forgot that anything was wrong. Then she would
look up accidentally and notice how he sat, limp and
heavy-limbed, not bothering to protect himself from the
net of words she had wound around him. She would
break off and say, "Do you want something? Iced tea?"

"No."

"Are you not sleeping nights?"

"I'm sleeping fine. Go on talking."

"How can I talk if I never get an answer? You talk
to *me*. What's been happening? Have you been back to
see your mother?"

"No."

"Are you going?"

"No."

"She can't still be angry with you."

"I don't care if she's angry or not, I'm not going."

"What, not *ever*?"

"I've had it," said Drum. "All this time telling how famous I'm going to be, and then she goes to pieces at one little setback. I'm nineteen years old. I got a right to get fired once, don't I? Oh, it looks like I will never get anywhere in this life. Never do a thing but bag groceries on Friday nights. A lot *she* cares."

"If you're not going back," said Evie, "where *are* you going?" She was careful about her tone of voice. Even a sudden movement, she felt, might frighten him away. But Drum only shook his head. He didn't seem to care what she said.

He spent five days moving between her house and David's, where he was allowed to visit but was not asked for meals. He shaved in the restroom of an Esso station, borrowed a change of clothes from David, and kept his guitar in David's tool shed. At Evie's house he saw only Evie and Clotelia. Once Violet came, pink-cheeked with curiosity after what Evie had told her on the phone, but Drum left immediately. "I believe he doesn't like me," Violet said.

"No, that's not it. It's some mood he's in," Evie told her. When Violet was there, she could draw back from things and see how strange they were: Evie Decker making excuses for a rock guitarist, protecting a fugitive sitting boldly in her kitchen chair. She said goodbye to Violet as soon as she could and went out back to signal toward the tall grass behind the house.

On Friday afternoon Drum's mother called. "This is Mrs. Ora Casey," she said stiffly. "Is that you, Evie?"

"Yes, ma'am," said Evie.

"I am trying to get ahold of Bertram. He's wandered off somewhere. Has he been by your house?"

"No, ma'am."

"If you see him, will you say I'm looking for him?"

"All right."

There was a pause.

"I've called David too," Mrs. Casey said. "*He's* not seen him. Now, where would a boy go off to like that?"

"Well, I'll certainly tell him you were looking for him."

"Evie, I'll be honest with you. I been looking for him all week now. Since Sunday. We had a little falling-out. Oh, it was all over nothing—a misunderstanding at the Parisian—but you know how sensitive he is. I told him he had let me down—well, I had my reasons. We may not be college-educated in our family but we are *law*-abiding, we don't give no one cause to complain about us. I did speak sharp to him, but only because I was disappointed, nothing permanent. What call did he have to take it to heart so?"

"Well, if I see him—" Evie said.

"Yes, yes. All right. Good-bye."

Evie hung up and went back to the living room, where Drum and Clotelia were watching soap operas. Drum had grown bolder now. When the television was on he sat watching it as if he were an invited guest, talking back to all the actors. "This here doctor," Clotelia was telling him, "think he's the center of the universe. Selfish? Watch." Drum nodded, probably not listening, concentrating on the screen so hard his eyes had turned to slits. He and Clotelia shared the couch. Clotelia had grown used to him, although she still said he was trash. "Now, here is what I want to know," she told him. "When that doctor mince in such a stuck-up way, is it *his* way? Or do he just act like that for the play? Which? Pull your gut in, Evie. Who was that on the phone?"

"No one," said Evie.

"If I don't get on her tail," Clotelia told Drum, "she would go around looking like a old bedsheet. What am I going to do? I tell my boyfriend, 'Brewster,' I say, 'you ain't going to believe it, but I know a white girl seventeen years old need a full-time nursemaid. Maid ain't enough,' I say. 'She need a nursemaid.' ''

Drum rolled his head back on the couch and watched Clotelia. During commercials he would listen to anyone. It didn't have to be Evie.

" 'Why won't you quit then?' he say. I tell him I will. Nothing more disgraceful, he say, than me spending my lifetime picking up over Evie Decker.''

"I wish you *would* quit," Evie said.

"Oh, I will, miss, I will." She made a face and twisted her watch around sharply. "Week to week I say I will. Only if I could find me something else to do. Factory job. Do you know how long I wasted on her? Four years. Now I got to say it was all for nothing and quit. My land."

"Go to some city, why don't you," Drum said.

"Sure. Be glad to."

"I would too, if I had the money."

Evie stood above him, folding her hands on the back of the couch and looking down at the top of his head. There was no part in his hair, just a dense sheet of black separating into thick strings. Sometimes, watching him sprawled in her house, she felt an unpleasant sense of surprise hit her. There were things about him that kept startling her each time she noticed them: the bony, scraped look of his wrists, the nicotine stain on his middle finger, the straggling hairs that edged his sideburns. He was sunk into the couch cushions as if he were permanent. If her father walked in right now, what would Drum do? Raise his hand no more than an inch, probably, say "Hey" and let the hand drop again.

"Drum Casey, what do you want from me?" she asked him.

"Huh?"

"What do you want, I said. Why are you hanging around here?"

"Evie, well, I never," Clotelia said.

Drum had turned to face her, with his mouth slightly open. "Well, if *that's* the way you feel," he said.

"I didn't say one word about the way I feel. I asked you a question."

"Some question."

"Well, have you ever been known to answer one? Have you ever had a real conversation, one that goes back and forth like it's supposed to? I asked you something. I want to know. What do you want out of me?"

"Watch now," Clotelia said loudly. "The lady in black going to cry; she's cried every show. How do you reckon she makes tears spurt that way?"

"It's fake, it's only water," said Drum. He stood up. "Talk like this just gets me down. If you don't like me sleeping on your porch, come out and say so. None of this roundaboutness."

"*Porch*? Who said porch? I asked you—"

"I got ears, I can hear."

"I wonder more about that every day," Evie said.

But Drum was already leaving, stuffing his cigarettes into his shirt pocket as he crossed the hallway. "So long," he said.

"Well, wait a minute—"

She saw his back as he loped down the front steps. Anyone could have seen him. Her father could have run into him on the sidewalk. When he reached the street he paused for a minute and then turned to the right, where he was half hidden by the hedge that bordered the yard. "I don't see you running after him," Clotelia told the television.

"I don't know if I wanted to," Evie said.

9

She lay awake most of the night, listening for the creak of the swing. It never came. In the morning when she got up she seemed to have returned to the way she was a week ago, brisk and cheerful, willingly sitting on a board while her father sawed it and then humming while she washed the dishes, since it was Clotelia's day off. But toward noon she grew restless. She followed her father aimlessly while he built shelves in the kitchen. Once she pointed to his work pants and said, "Are you going to wear *those* all day?"

"What's wrong with them?"

"Well, if you're going out, I mean. Aren't you going downtown?"

"No, I hadn't planned on it."

"Tomorrow's Sunday, you know."

"Was there something you needed?"

"Oh, no," Evie said.

She went out into the back yard and sat on the steps, looking toward the field of grass where Drum used to wait. Nothing moved. She sat there for hours, for an entire afternoon, without so much as a book in her lap. Her eyes began to sting from staring at one place so steadily.

After supper she went outside again, this time to the front porch. Neighbors' televisions blared up and down

the street. From the window behind her she heard her
father's shortwave radio flicking rapidly across conti-
nents. "Evie, come here, I've got Moscow," he called
once. And then, a little later, "There is too much Spanish in this world." Evie picked up a cushion and set it
in her lap. It smelled musty, like the inside of an old
summer cottage. If every evening lasted this long, how
much time would it take to get her whole life lived?
Centuries. She pictured herself growing older and fatter
in this airless dark house, turning into a spinster with a
pouched face and a zipper of lines across her upper lip,
caring for her father until he died and she had no one
left but cats or parakeets.

Her father went to bed with a book. Lights blinked
off up and down the street, and chairs were scraped off
porches through bright yellow doors that finally closed
and darkened. Then someone came up the sidewalk, all
alone. She watched him swing over the hedge and cut
across the lawn to the front porch steps. "Oh, you know
better than anyone, don't you?" he said.

"Know what?"

"How come you're sitting out here? You're waiting
for me to slink back, nowhere else to go."

He climbed the steps and sank down on the swing,
at the opposite end from her. "Everybody asked about
you," he said.

"Who do you mean?"

"At the Unicorn."

"I thought you weren't going there this week," Evie
said.

"No call not to, is there? Sure we did. Last night
and tonight, same as ever. People said, 'Where is that
girl who cut herself up, has she found her someone else
by now?' I was thinking of saying you had killed your-

self. 'Finished what she started,' I would say. *That* would have gone big.''

"You don't know what you're talking about," Evie said. "Do you think I would kill myself over the likes of you?"

"Then I went back home with David and slept in the tool shed. His mother came out in the morning with a broom. Old witch, should have been riding it. 'What are *you* doing here?' she asks. I swear if she wasn't about to sweep me right out."

"Well, I don't blame her," Evie said. "You just hang on and *hang* on, Drum Casey. When are you going to leave me alone? As soon as I get used to you being gone, you turn up again. Will you ever just get out and stay out?"

"Oh, now, don't make me go," said Drum. "It's late. I'm tired."

"Well, so am I."

She drew in her breath, waiting for him to say something else that she could fire back at him, but he seemed to have given up. He sat slumped against the arm of the swing. All she saw was a black shadow with his T shirt making a triangle of white above his jacket. Finally he said, "You know Joseph Ballew? He says, 'Where is that plump girl with "Casey" on her forehead? Lost her interest? You're slipping, man,' he says."

Evie didn't answer.

"Have you ever thought of losing some weight?"

It took a moment for his words to sink in. Then she said, "Well, my God in heaven."

"Have you?"

"Why do you feel free to act so rude? I eat less than *you* do."

"I was just asking. You know, in Tar City they got

this slenderizing place. Steam baths and exercise machines. You ever been to one?"

"No, I have not."

"Well. This girl was telling about it. Seems they can really slim people down. And make-up, and hair styles— You know, I saw in this magazine once where they decide the shape of your face and then fix your hair to fit it. They had before-and-after pictures; it looked real good."

"I wish you would go," Evie said.

"What, *now*?"

"Nobody *makes* you sit here. If you can't stand my looks, find someone else's porch to sleep on."

"Well, wait now," Drum said. "You got it all wrong. I'm trying to help out."

"I didn't ask for any help."

"I just want you to look your best. There's no reason you should get mad about it."

"What business is it of yours if I look my best?"

"Well, I was thinking we might could get married," Drum said.

Evie held still for a minute, not breathing. Then she began to laugh.

"Did I say something funny?" Drum asked.

"Yes," she said. But the laugh, which should have flowed on, suddenly rusted and broke. "I believe you're out of your head," she said.

"Why? Don't you want to?"

"No, I don't," said Evie.

"I don't know what you got to lose. You must like me some or you wouldn't have, you know, cut the letters. You wouldn't hang around me all the time. And here I am with no home. And my career's at a standstill, we could get our pictures in the papers. Human interest. Plus I do like you. I wouldn't be asking if I didn't."

"What do you like about me?" Evie said.

"Jesus."

"Well, go on. Name something."

"*I* don't know. I like the way you listen to people. Is that enough?"

"No," said Evie.

"Look. I like you. I want to get married. I feel like things are just petering out all around me and I want to get married to someone I like and have me a house and *change*. Make a change. Isn't that enough? Don't you want to change your life around some?"

Evie held the cushion closer to her and breathed in its musty smell. Then she lifted a hand and ran one finger across her forehead, tracing the narrow ridges of the scars, which always felt pleasantly crinkled. In the opposite house, the last of the lights went out. People slept fitfully in hot, rumpled beds hollowed to fit their shapes, in houses they had grown up and grown old in. Beside her, Drum shifted in the swing. He was waiting for her answer, which would be yes, but only after she had taken her time over it. Things moved too fast. She had wanted a courtship, with double dates and dances and matching shirts, but all she got was three minutes of staring at sleeping houses before she said, "Oh, well. Why not?" and Drum slid over to kiss her with cool blank lips.

10

She awoke from a dream in which she slipped through slimy clay, trying to escape a reckless woman driver in an army car. It was nearly ten o'clock in the morning. The second hand of her alarm clock spun off circle after circle while she lay watching, unable to move her eyes or gather her thoughts together. A steeple bell rang. The Sunday paper slapped against the screen. Her father passed her door on his way to church, and she wondered if he would find Drum asleep in the swing. But even that was not enough to unfasten her eyes from the clock.

Long after her father's car had driven off, she heard the front door slam. Drum's boots crossed the down-stairs hall. "You there?" he called.

Evie didn't answer.

"Evie?"

"All right, I'm coming," Evie said.

Lying still so long without breakfast had made her dizzy. Black and blue buttons swarmed toward her when she climbed out of bed. As soon as her eyes had cleared she stepped into last night's clothes and then went to the mirror to unravel her pincurls. How would she curl her hair if she were married? Clotelia's magazines said no man liked to see his wife in curlers. The word "wife" hit her strangely, stilling her fingers for a moment. It was more definite than "married," which had merely floated shapelessly in her mind since the night before. She saw herself in a housecoat, mixing orange juice; saying no to a vacuum-cleaner salesman; wondering if it were time to start supper. None of the situations seemed likely. What Drum had come for, she thought, was to tell her he had changed his mind. She would never be a wife, after all. She felt so certain of it that she descended the stairs blank-faced, shut against everything, and when she saw him lounging in the living room doorway she failed to smile.

But all Drum said was, "Could you fix some breakfast?"

"All right," she said.

She fried eggs and bacon while he leaned on the stove and watched. The shut feeling was still with her, causing a brisk competence which she had never had before. Eggs plopped neatly in the frying pan, and she laid down strips of bacon in exactly parallel lines. Then Drum said, "No biscuits?"

"You'll have to do without," she told him. "I don't know how to make them."

"Can't you get Clotelia to show you? Breakfast is not breakfast without no biscuits."

"Clotelia isn't here today."

"I mean later. For the future. I'm used to having biscuits every morning."

"Oh. Later," Evie said. She let out a long breath and laid the spatula on the stove top. "Well, sure, I guess so."

"That's the girl," Drum said.

She left him to eat his breakfast alone while she fried more eggs for herself. She had turned hungry suddenly. While the eggs popped and sputtered in the frying pan, Drum finished everything on his plate, sopping it up with slice after slice of white bread. "I've got the Jeep tomorrow," he said with his mouth full.

"You do?"

"David's lending it to me. I asked him this morning. We can drive to South Carolina and be back in time for supper."

"South *Carolina*?"

Drum looked up from his plate. "What's the matter?" he said. "Did you forget all about it? Last night you said you would run off with me. I was counting on it."

"But South Carolina. I can't go there."

"Why not?"

"Well, Dillon, you mean. Where everybody goes when they have to get married, all the trash goes. You expect me to run off to *Dillon*?"

"Well, sure," said Drum.

"No, we have to go somewhere else."

"But there ain't nowhere else. Dillon's the only place you don't have to wait for three days."

"I'm sorry, I just can't help it," said Evie. Which was exactly what she meant; she had had no idea that she was going to object to Dillon. Words popped forth ready-made, strung from her mouth like comic-strip balloons. "I would rather wait for the license, even. Anything. Do you think I want to go around the rest of my life with a South Carolina marriage certificate? Oh, you just have no *respect*, Drum Casey."

"Well, my Lord," said Drum.

"Besides, we'd have to lie about my age anyway. Even in Dillon. We might as well do it in Tar City, or Raleigh."

"We'd have to lie *more* in Tar City," said Drum. "I would be underage too, if we went there."

"I don't care."

"They'd ask for proof. Then where would we be?"

"I don't care."

She waited to see what she would say next, but nothing more came. And there sat Drum, tapping a cigarette against his thumbnail over and over until the tobacco had settled a good eighth of an inch, but still he didn't light it. He would be framing a way to say, "All right, then. Stay home. Die an old maid." He was joined to her by a piece of elastic which she had stretched too far. With Drum, even an inch was too far. "I know what you must be thinking," she told him. "I'm sorry, I really meant that. But can't you go along with me this once? I'll never ask you again."

"Oh, well. Shoot," said Drum. Then he finally struck a match, but her father's car was just driving up. He had to leave by the back door, hunching his shoulders and cupping the match flame as he went.

"Evie," her father said, "why do I smell smoke?"

"Well, I've taken up cigarettes," Evie said.

"I thought so. Just so you are straightforward about it, then. I know young people have to try these things."

"All right," Evie said.

"I was young myself once," said her father.

It was Violet who helped most with the arrangements. ("*Eloping?*" she had said. "Evie. Aren't you excited? Oh, and here I thought this Drum business was all in your head.") She investigated marriage laws, arranged for the blood tests, chauffeured them to the doctor in her mother's convertible. "As far as the license goes," she said, "lie. Don't bother pulling out phony documents and such, lie through your teeth. You'd be amazed how much you can get away with." She drove Evie to Tar City to apply for the license, and Evie lied and no one questioned her. All the way home Violet sang "O Promise Me," causing people to slow down and stare as they passed. Planning things seemed to turn Violet larger and more brightly colored. She took up over half of the car seat, and every time she thought of how they had fooled the clerk she laughed her lazy rich laugh. Meanwhile Evie sat in the corner with her hands between her knees. She pictured Tar City policemen swooping down on them to hand a summons through the window for perjury, or the clerk having second thoughts and alerting all ministers and J.P.'s, or her father coming out front to point at Violet's car and say, "That's Tar *City* dust on those wheels. What have you been up to in Tar City?" But the ride home was smooth and quick, and when she went in Clotelia didn't even look up from the television.

They had to wait three days after they applied for the license. During that whole time it rained, breaking the heat wave and pulling the town from its stupor. Evie kept finding Drum on the back doorstep, under the eaves, huddled into David's windbreaker to keep warm. She pulled him in whenever her father wasn't around, but once they were sitting side by side they had almost nothing to say to each other. Drum discussed houses. He had heard of a cheap one for rent, twenty-four dollars a month. When he had finished with that, Evie went over and over the details of applying for the license, as if that were the one solid link that would hold them together till Thursday. "The clerk said, 'Date of birth?' I had it all worked out beforehand, but still I thought I would slip. Where I did slip was your name. 'Drum Casey,' I said. 'No, Bertram.' I must have sounded half-witted, not knowing the name of my, of the boy."

"I reckon so," said Drum.

They were quiet for a minute. He was beside her on the couch, one arm draped across her shoulders and his hand dangling free.

"They wanted to know your mother's maiden name," said Evie. "Did I tell you that? I made one up. What was your mother's maiden name?"

"I don't know. Parker."

"I forget what I told them. Maybe Parker, after all.

Wouldn't that be funny? I had to think even for *my* mother's maiden name, which shows you how flustered I was. Eve Abbott: my own first two names. It should have been on the tip of my tongue.''

When Clotelia was far enough away Drum would pull Evie closer, choosing the first pause in her speech. Evie had been waiting to be kissed for years. She had rehearsed it in her mind, first with someone faceless and then with Drum, who looked as if he would know all about it; but now she didn't think it was what it had been built up to be. They stayed pressed together between kisses, looking out over each other's shoulders like drivers meeting on opposite lanes of a highway. Drum smelled like tobacco and marigolds and the flattened porch cushions, which had turned mustier than ever now that the rain was here.

On Thursday, she got up early and put on a white eyelet dress that she had saved from junior-high graduation. The seams had grayed and it was a little tight, but she had set her heart on white. She filled her purse with absolute necessities, in case her father told her never to darken his door again: make-up, two diaries, all the letters received since fifth grade, a photograph of her parents taken before she was born, and a billfold containing twenty-eight dollars. Then she tiptoed out of the house. Her father was still dressing. Just as she reached the stairs she heard him slam a drawer and say, "Oh, drat." It surprised her that she could do something so momentous without his sensing it.

She set out for a corner halfway between her house and Violet's, where Drum and David were going to pick them up. ("If Violet's coming, then so is David," Drum said. "I ain't going to be outnumbered"—as if this were some sort of contest, girls against boys.) The rain had stopped, but the streets still glistened and the lawns were a dark, shiny green. She edged puddles not yet dried by the sun and hopped across flowing gutters, feeling like a star in an old movie with her high heels clacking so importantly and her full skirt swirling around her calves. On the corner where they were to meet, Violet was already waiting. She wore a pink nylon cocktail dress. "I believe this is the most exciting day of my life," she called out. Evie hushed her. She was certain someone would notice them and guess what was happening.

They waited five minutes. Evie stared very hard in a direction away from where the Jeep would be coming. When she heard it pull up behind her, she began smiling widely and couldn't stop. "Hop in," David said. Evie climbed into the back, where Violet was already settling herself. She looked steadily eastward so that the smile would be taken for a squint against the sunlight. Up front Drum sat lounging in the corner of her eye, one of his feet resting on the dashboard. He wore a white shirt with his jeans and his hair was slicked down too neatly. David was dressed the same as always—a sign of protest, it turned out. He was against the wedding. In all these days of planning Evie had never thought to ask how David felt, and it took her a minute to understand when he said, "All right, here we go. But it's against my better judgment, I just want you to know."

"You already said that," Drum told him.

"He did?" Evie said. She sat forward and looked at the back of David's neck. "Said what? He thinks we shouldn't be getting married?"

"Damn right I do," said David. "There is something too half-baked about this deal. And besides. Here I am. His manager. Aren't I supposed to know what's good for him? Careerwise, marriage is suicide. Look at the Beatles."

"*I* still like the Beatles," Violet said.

"But you don't swoon away when you hear them, now, do you?"

"I never did," Violet said.

That ended the conversation. For the rest of the ride everyone sat in his own corner, staring out at the scenery. Evie's smile had faded. She watched tobacco barns zip by, each standing out bare and lonely along the flat highway. Men in filling stations turned their blank faces slowly to follow the Jeep out of sight. Barefoot children strung across the pavement drew in while they passed and then fanned out again.

When they reached the outskirts of the city, the buildings tightened together. They pressed Evie's heart out of rhythm; she kept clearing her throat and swallowing. All around them people were busy with humdrum things, waiting for buses or driving the groceries home, bearing loads of children and picnic baskets and diaper bags to some sunny playground. They sped by in small circles of cheerfulness, with Evie watching enviously until they were too tiny to see.

When they were nearly downtown, they stopped for a red light. A very short fat man with a child's face stepped up to wipe their windshield, using a greasy cloth. He smeared the dirt around and stepped back to wait for a tip, but David only scowled at him. And still the light didn't change. They were going to wait there forever, eye to eye with a watchful little man. "Oh, I tell you," David said. "Everything has gone wrong today, everything. I can't wait to see what'll happen to me next."

"Name one thing that has gone wrong," Violet said. "Other than that man," she added, for by then the light had changed and they were pulling away.

"Isn't it enough that we are heading for Drum's wedding? I'm driving my own hearse wagon, I don't know why I do it. Inside of a month he'll be a full-time pump attendant and I'll be out of a job. And *you*," he said, nodding to Evie in the rear-view mirror, "don't look at me like that. It's your own good I'm thinking of, partly."

Evie didn't argue with him. None of it seemed real anyway. Time was speeding up and slowing down in fits, like her pulse. The argument between David and Violet moved as rapidly as a silent film, jumping so suddenly into anger that Evie felt she must have missed a whole section of it. "Where is your *tact*?" Violet was asking. "We are here to get my girl friend married, it's the happiest day of her life, and you sit talking about hearse wagons. Well, stop right here. Let us out. We'll *walk* to the wedding."

"Tact, nothing," said David. "It's a free country, ain't it? I got a right to voice an opinion just like anybody else."

"Voice it by yourself, then. We three are walking."

"Go ahead," David said. "But let me tell you one thing, fat girl. I didn't like you the moment I set eyes on you. Organize, organize, I know you like a book. Why don't you get something of your *own* to organize?" He stopped the car with a jolt and reached across Drum to open the door. "Get out, all that wants to. You won't hurt my feelings a bit."

"Fine," Violet said. "Pick us up at the nearest J.P., in an hour."

"Minister," Evie told her. "And anyway—"

"Minister, then. I don't care. You just go have yourself a beer, David Elliott."

"What?" said Drum. He had been watching pedestrians all this time, not appearing to listen, but now he turned halfway in his seat and raised his dark glasses. "*Minister*, what's that for? What's wrong with J.P.?"

"Well, nothing," said Evie. "Only I was always hoping, well, I was counting on a minister. Also a church."

Violet nodded.

"What next," David said.

"Things are getting out of hand here," said Drum. "I had never looked for all *this*."

"Well, now's the time to back out," David told him.

Violet said, "Will you just *hush*? Evie, climb out. We're walking."

"No, wait," Evie said.

"Do you want him to ruin your wedding?"

"It'll be ruined for sure if you walk," said Drum. "Because *I* ain't coming."

"Wait," Evie said.

Time slowed to its regular pace. Everyone hushed and stared at her.

"Nobody walks," she told them. "I plan to have a normal, ordinary wedding, with witnesses who aren't called in off the street. No fighting. No disapproving. We are going to do this one thing the way it ought to be done, and afterwards we will have a bottle of wine to celebrate. Now, is that too much to ask?"

"Well—" said Violet.

"All right. Shut the door," Drum said. "Looks like we got to find us a minister."

"Methodist," Evie said.

The minister had a face she forgot an hour later. He perched, childlike, on the edge of his seat when they drove him to his church, and he stayed that way forever in Evie's mind. All she remembered of the wedding itself was the smell of musty swing cushions when Drum stood beside her at the altar. For souvenirs she had a wire-thin ring and a marriage certificate in old English lettering, two engraved doves cuddling at its head and David and Violet's ball-point signatures on the witness lines.

11

For twenty-four dollars a month they rented a tar-paper shack on the outskirts of Pulqua. A series of tenant farmers had once lived there. Tobacco fields stretched away from it on all sides, and the gravel road in front was traveled by barefoot children and mule wagons. Evie thought it was a wonderful place to start out in. The tenant farmers had been too poor to leave even a strip of carpeting or a one-eared sugar bowl; the house was blank, waiting for Evie to make her mark. Nothing she could do would hurt it.

She plastered the papery walls with posters advertising the Unicorn. She spent eighteen dollars at the dimestore, entering the amount carefully in a budget book, and lugged home tea towels and cutlery and a set of dishes the bluish color of skim milk. Their furniture came from Evie's father's house. They had moved it in a U-Haul-It the afternoon of the wedding, because they couldn't afford a night in a motel.

First her father said, "Married?" Then he sat down on the porch steps and said, "Married. I don't believe it." He was slumped and hollow-faced, exposed before Drum and David and Violet, whom Evie had brought, without thinking, up the front walk with her. They stood in a semicircle around him and frowned at the ground. "Have you ever met Drum?" Evie asked finally.

"No, I don't believe I have," her father said. He rose and held his hand out, not quite looking into Drum's eyes. He could have threatened annulment, but he didn't. He didn't seem to have the energy to think it up.

"And this is David Elliott," Evie told him. "Violet you know."

But her father wasn't paying attention.

"Are you the rock singer?" he asked Drum.

"Yes, sir."

"Casey."

"Yes, sir."

"Well, I don't understand. I was going to take her to a plastic surgeon; none of this was necessary."

"Sir?"

"Oh, it's all beyond me," Evie's father said.

"Mr. Decker," said Drum, "Evie and I will need furniture. Do you reckon we could borrow what you have extra?"

"Well," said her father. He turned and went into the house. Would he lock the door behind him, say he never wanted to set eyes upon them again? But when he was inside he said, "Take what you want, then. Evie will show you."

"Thank you, sir," Drum said.

His mother was different. She clutched at Drum's shoulders and said, "You *what*? You fool. What would make you go and do a thing like that?" And Evie stood in the doorway, wondering where to put her hands. She hadn't wanted to come in the first place. "You said you were never going back," she had told Drum. "Why now? Why drag me with you?"

"Because I want to show her I'm settled and done with her," Drum said.

He stood motionless in his mother's grip, although

she was trying to shake him. "It was you always telling
me I didn't appreciate her," he said.

"Well, I didn't mean *marry* her."

"It's done now. Do we have to get in a swivet over
it?"

"In a swivet, you say. My life is broke in pieces and
you tell me not to get in a swivet. You, Evie Decker.
Don't you look at me so smug. I'll get every lawyer in
town after you. I'll annul it, I'll have your marriage
license tore up by the highest judge there is. Oh, where
is your father when I need him the most?"

She grabbed the hand of one of Drum's little towheaded brothers, who shifted his feet and grinned.

Drum said, "Mom, can I have the record player from
my room?"

Who would have thought that Drum Casey would be so
homey? He wanted cushions for all the chairs and curtains for the windows, a checkered skirt for the stilt-
legged kitchen sink and a frilly bibbed apron for Evie.
During the first three days they were married he spent
his time installing can openers, toothbrush holders, and
towel rods. He directed their settling in as if he had had
in mind, for years, a blueprint for a home of his own
complete to the last detail. "That easy chair goes in the
bedroom, for when I'm making up songs. No more lying around on a bed to play my guitar. The other chair
goes in the corner of the living room. We want our
furniture in corners. We want to sit snug in corners
when we're home of an evening. Do you know how to
make biscuits yet?"

Evie paid a call on Clotelia, choosing nighttime so
that she could go to Clotelia's own house instead of her
father's. "Well, look who's here," said Clotelia, kick-

ing open the screen door. "The girl with the peabrain, I declare."

"I came to see how to make baking-powder biscuits," Evie said.

"Ain't you got no cookbook?"

"You know a cookbook wouldn't do it right. Drum has a special recipe in mind."

"Sure. Him and his kind use bacon drippings," said Clotelia. "Nothing special to *that*. Oh, come on in."

She led Evie through the darkened living room, where an old woman with powder-puff hair sat nodding on a vinyl couch. In the kitchen, she sat Evie on a step-stool decaled with panda bears. She whipped up a mound of crumbling dough, mixing it with quick, angry fingers and cutting it out with a drinking glass before Evie even realized it was finished. Meanwhile Evie stared around her to see how other people's kitchens were kept. "What is that china thing on your stove?" she asked.

"Spoon-rest."

"Oh, I see."

"Cost me fifteen cents at a rummage sale."

"Well, that's the trouble. Fifteen cents here, a quarter there—you don't know how they add up. *I* didn't know."

"Should have thought of that before you got married," Clotelia said.

"Why are you talking like this? I thought you had started liking Drum."

"I tell you why: go look at your father. You've broke his heart."

"You never cared before how he felt."

"Nor don't now," said Clotelia, "but it kills me to see somebody's heart broke. When you going to visit him?"

"Well, maybe in a day or two."

"All right. You got your recipe; important thing is
mix it with your fingers. Now go before Brewster
comes. You know he don't like to see you here.''

She fanned Evie out the door with floury hands.
Drum was waiting for her in David's Jeep, with a crowd
of little boys closing in like moths to touch the headlights and run their fingers over the canvas top. "Shoo
now,'' Drum told them. "You get the recipe?''

"I think so,'' Evie said.

He drove her home carefully, as if the recipe were
something precious and she the shell that held it.

On Wednesday school began. She went, even though
Drum couldn't see the point. "*I* never finished, and I
ain't sorry, either,'' he said.

"But it's silly to quit my senior year.''

"All right, suit yourself.''

There was Mr. Harrison to argue with too. He was
the principal, a close friend of her father's, but even so
he had to tell her about the rule against married students. "We make exceptions, sure,'' he said. "Especially when their grades are as good as yours. But not
if you, not if there's a little one on the way, so to
speak.''

"No, of course not,'' Evie said.

"And then too, it would depend on your discretion.
We have a lot of impressionable young girls here. Knowing you as I do, I'm sure you wouldn't *talk* about, well,
but still—''

"Of course not,'' Evie said again.

Even if she did talk, what would she say? She had
overheard more in the girls' gym than she had yet found
out with Drum in the papery bedroom. Their love-
making was sudden and awkward, complicated by pitch
dark and a twisted nightgown and the welter of sheets
and blankets that Evie kept covering herself with. Be-

sides, there weren't many people she could talk *to*. She
arrived every morning at the last minute, having caught
a Trailways bus out on the highway and ridden it in to
the drugstore terminal. In class, people stared at her
and were too polite. She didn't mind. She had known
that getting married would set her apart. And there was
always Violet, who ate at her table in the cafeteria and
walked her to the drugstore after school. Violet was full
of talk. Witnessing a wedding seemed to have the same
effect as being godmother at a christening: she was pro-
prietary, enthusiastic. "Evie! Do you *cook*, just like
that, every night without a single lesson? Does he like
what you feed him? Have you had your first quarrel?
Oh, I can't wait till I'm married. Nights when I pass
lighted houses I think, 'All those people, so cozy with
someone they belong to, and here I am alone.' I think
you're the luckiest girl in the senior class."

Coziness, that must be what the world was all about.
It was what Violet wanted, and David, who sank onto
their borrowed couch and kicked off his shoes and said,
"Oh, man, a place all your own. I might get married
myself someday." And most of all it was what Drum
wanted, when he rolled over in bed to watch her dress
and said, "Ah, *don't* go to school. Stay home and make
me pancakes. I'll do more for you than any schoolhouse
will."

"But we're getting ready for a test."

"So what? It's cold outside. Stay in the house where
it's warm."

And often she did, more and more as fall set in and
the fields were frosted over every morning. Drum
worked very little now—just odd jobs at the A & P, and
then the two evenings at the Unicorn. If she stayed home
their days were unscheduled and almost motionless,
with great blocks of time spent on manufactured tasks.

Afternoons, Drum practiced his guitar or made up songs. He tested new lyrics in a mumble, almost inaudible—*"My girl's wearing patent leather shoes—"* No. *"My girl wears—"* The guitar strings barely tinkled. At first Evie stayed in the other room, thinking she might get on his nerves, but eventually he would crash down on all the strings at once and say, "Where are you? What are you doing out *there*, come in and keep me company." Then she sat on the edge of the bed, watching how the slant of his black hair fell over the guitar just as it had the first night she saw him.

She worried that he would get tired of her. She spent weeks feeling she had to walk on tiptoe and check everything for stupidity before she said it, since she had never imagined that Drum would settle quickly into being married. He would be hard to live with, she had thought. She had seen his moody silences and the way he shrugged off what people said to him. But he turned out to be the easiest person she knew. All he wanted was a wife. He ate what she fed him, kept her company when she washed the dishes, slept with one arm thrown across her chest, and rose in the morning asking for her baking-powder biscuits. Gradually she stopped tiptoeing. She talked about anything that came to mind—a casserole in *The Ladies' Home Journal* or a new way to stop runs in stockings—and he kept cheerfully silent and mended chairs. These were the things she was *supposed* to talk about. Wearing her bibbed apron, tying a scarf over her pincurls, she began to feel as sure and as comfortable as any of the feather-light girls floating down high-school corridors.

"All I saw was a cat, slinking on a fence," Drum called out at the Unicorn.

"Will he be there tonight?"

"Yeah!" his audience said.

"Will I *be there tonight?"*

He wore black. He was cool and glittering. Evie sat smiling below him in a baggy brown skirt and a sweater that rode up around her waist.

"My girl is at a hymn-sing.

"What happened to double ferris wheels?"

"Yeah!" they said again.

She still couldn't understand what that speaking out was about.

She had to darn socks now instead of throwing them away, and she clipped recipes for meatless meals and carried her lunch to school in a brown paper bag. They never paid the rent on time. "There is nothing for it," said Drum, "but to get me a part-time job. I wish now I hadn't fallen out with my daddy. Pumping gas was not too enjoyable but the pay was sure good, and where else would they let me work such loose hours?"

"Make peace with him, then," Evie said.

"I don't much feel like it."

"Well, I didn't say apologize. Just get on speaking terms. We'll have them to dinner with my father, settle all this family business at one sitting."

"Nah, it'd never work out," Drum said.

"We could give it a try, though."

She set the dinner for the second Sunday in November. That Friday in school she invited her father, choosing one of those moments when they met in the hall and stood awkwardly searching for something to say. Then she telephoned Drum's mother from the drugstore. "Thank you, but we'll not trouble you by coming," Mrs. Casey said, and hung up. Evie dialed again. The receiver was lifted on the first ring. "Mrs. Casey, we were *expecting* you," Evie said. That was the only argument she could think of, but it seemed to be enough. "Oh, well, then," Mrs. Casey said, "I reckon we can fit it in. I don't believe in letting people down."

Evie fixed a casserole a full day ahead: tuna fish and canned peas. Early Sunday morning she washed all the ash trays and filmed them with floor wax, the way *Good Housekeeping* had told her to. She refused to let Drum use them after that; he had to carry around a Mason jar lid. "This is getting on my nerves," he said. "Can't you just *relax*?"

But she couldn't. She worried that her father might be dismayed by the house, or that Mrs. Casey would start a fight. All these weeks she had been half expecting an annulment to come through (a scroll of parchment, she pictured it, stamped with the state seal and *"Esse quam videri,"* arriving in a mailing tube to prove that she was nobody's wife after all) and now she wondered if Mrs. Casey planned to bring it in person. "Here. A little housewarming gift." She remembered exactly the flowing tone of Mrs. Casey's voice, soft but pushing steadily forward, and the rhythm it set up with the other voices trying to survive beside it. What if an argument started somehow between Mrs. Casey and Evie's father? Her father would be beaten to the ground. She straightened the table settings nervously, stood back to squint at them, and then straightened them again.

Her father arrived first. When she opened the door to him he stood folded into his thin overcoat with his hands in his pockets. He entered stooping, as if he were coming to inspect a child's playhouse. "Well," he said. "So this is where you live." Then he smiled and kissed her, looking at the floor.

"Do you like it?" Evie asked him.

"It's a little cold, isn't it?"

"No, it's very comfortable."

"What do you use for heat?"

"We have a very good oil stove. There, see? Over there."

"Oh, yes," said her father. But he still didn't look.

Then Drum's parents came, and Drum appeared from the bedroom buttoning his shirt cuffs. He stood still while his mother kissed him on one cheek. Mrs. Casey wore a feathered hat and a rayon dress with a draped bosom; Mr. Casey was in a blue suit and white spectator shoes. He was sharp-boned and whiskery, with very round bright eyes. Nothing like Drum. Evie had never seen him before, but instead of introducing them Mrs. Casey just tipped her head toward him and he nodded gravely. "We like to got lost," Mrs. Casey said. "Well. I was *wondering* what kind of house you all had. My, it surely is—I understand you teach, Mr. Decker." The neckline of her dress pouched outward, framing a V of skin reddened by the constant pinching motion of her fingers. Gardenia perfume powdered the air around her. She carried no documents.

At dinner they all outdid each other in compliments and small courtesies. They circulated serving dishes, spoon side outward; they leapt to pass the butter to whoever asked for it and they filled silences with hopeful questions. Like salesmen, they over-used each other's names. "Mr. Decker, have you lived in Farinia all your life?" "Evie tells me you run a service station, Mr. Casey." "Do you bowl, Mr. Decker?" Meanwhile Evie watched anxiously as her food disappeared into people's mouths, and Drum ate in silence with his face calm and distant.

The only tension was over the contest to be best-behaved. Evie's father won. He said, "Evie, Drum, I'm giving you a late wedding present. Well, nothing very fancy, but I'm buying myself a new car. Would you like the VW?"

"Boy. Sure would," said Drum. "We got the devil's own time getting anywhere."

"That's what I thought. I know that Evie isn't, doesn't keep a perfect attendance record these days. Not that it's any of my business, but I figured a car might help."

"Thank you, Daddy," Evie said. The afternoon was too perilous to bother arguing about her attendance record. Her father sat with his fingers together, the tip of his nose whitening as it always did under strain. Mrs. Casey was pleating the V of skin again.

"Lord knows we don't have extra cars to hand out," she said, "or anything like that; we're only simple folk. But your daddy here was thinking you might want your old job back, Bertram. Plenty would give their right arms for that job."

"Well, I could use it, I reckon," Drum said. "Sure."

The three parents sat side by side, keeping their backs very straight, as if the couch were something breakable.

At three o'clock they left. Mrs. Casey said, "Well, I surely did—Obed, where is my purse? Now, don't be a stranger, Bertram. You come by whenever you like—even if you just get lonesome, or hungry for a snack. Thank you for the sweet lunch, Evie."

"Joyed it," said Mr. Casey.

Evie's father carefully buttoned all the buttons of his coat. He kissed Evie on the cheek and shook Drum's hand. "My car will be coming next Wednesday," he said. "Thursday I'll give you the keys to the VW. Won't you come by and see me sometime?"

"Oh, of course," said Evie. "It's just that these last few weeks have been so busy. Getting settled and all."

"You could come for supper some night. Will you do that?"

"Of course," Evie said.

She stood beside Drum in the doorway, shivering

slightly, watching the two cars grow smaller. "Now," Drum said. "It's over and done with."

She nodded.

"And hot dog, we got us a car. Ain't that something? I always did like stick-shifts."

"I believe that's all you can think about," Evie said.

"Huh?"

"Well, you could at least have said thank you. Or talked to him more. Oh, I know that car, it smells woolly like his school suit and I will think about that every time I get in it. Couldn't you just tell him you appreciated it?"

"Nothing wrong with a woolly smell," said Drum.

"No," Evie said, giving up. So when he suddenly tightened his arms around her, pulling her close, it came as a surprise.

"Don't fret, I'm here," he said.

Beneath his shirt she felt his rib cage, thin and warm, and she heard the steady beating of his heart.

12

Then one Saturday at the Unicorn, Drum got into an argument. Not a fist fight, this time; just a shouting quarrel. It was almost midnight. Evie was splitting a burnt-out match into tiny slivers of paper while she waited for the evening to end, and the crowd had thinned enough so that she heard clearly when Drum's voice rose in the back room. "The hell you say. What you trying to pull, Zack?" She looked up, first toward the back room and then at the people sharing her table—three couples, talking softly over empty beer mugs, separated from other couples by a jungle of vacant chairs. None of them paid any attention. "Ah, don't give me *that*," Drum said. Evie rose and pushed through the chairs and behind the band platform. When she reached the back room she squinted in through layers of smoke. There was Drum, facing the proprietor and holding his guitar by the neck. David stood beside him. ". . . to be sensible about this, Drum," he was saying. Nearest Evie were Joseph Ballew and Joseph's bass player. "I don't see *Joseph* getting treated so light," Drum said.

"Joseph's our lead player," the proprietor told him. "You know that."

"Have you got some method to tell who draws in what people? No. All you got is—"

"Look, Drum, you'll still play on Saturdays. But Fridays, face it, there ain't all that big a crowd nowadays. You want me to lose money?"

"What's going on?" Evie asked.

They looked at her and then turned away again, not answering. Finally David said, "Zack was just saying how—"

"I been cut back to one night a week," said Drum. "There was a full house tonight and it's almost Christmas and now Zack here decides he's losing money."

"Now, Drum, if I could see my way clear you *know* I'd—" Zack said. He looked fatter than ever and very sad, with sweat running down the sides of his face like tears. "Spring, of course, we could see about having you for both nights again. It all goes by *seasons*, don't you see."

"He's right," said Joseph.

"*You* can talk," Drum told him. "How would you feel to get cut back without no warning?"

"Sure, I know how—"

"Ah, forget it," Drum said. "Where's my coat?"

"It's right behind you," Evie said.

But Drum went on stamping through the room, shoving chairs aside and looking under instrument cases. When finally he found the coat he said, "Another thing. You can forget Saturdays too, from now on. I ain't coming back here. You'll have to get along without me."

"Now, Drum, wait," said David.

"Do you want a ride or don't you?"

He pushed his way out of the room, right past Evie, and David looked at the others for a minute and then shrugged and followed him. Evie had to run to catch up with them.

Outside, the air was crackling with a sharp dry cold that made her ears tighten. She stumbled after Drum and David, struggling into her coat on the way. Their car was haloed with frost. While Drum unlocked the door Evie shifted from one foot to the other to keep warm, but Drum didn't look cold at all. He pulled the key out of the handle and then just stood there a minute, staring out over the icy roofs of other cars. "Hop in," David told Evie. "Let me sit up front. I'll talk to him."

Evie perched on the edge of the narrow back seat. One knee rested against Drum's guitar, which had kept some of the warmth from the Unicorn. While Drum was backing out no one spoke, but then on the highway Drum said, "Damn fat fool."

"He's just having to look out for his business," David said.

"What, over Christmas? School's letting out, the place'll be jammed. And how about Joseph, now? How does he get to stay?"

"Zack told you. Joseph is the—"

"All right, all right. The lead player. Who don't even have a sense of rhythm. I tell you, we're well out of that place. Got to find us something *lively* now."

"Well, where, Drum? Do you think you can pick up a new job just by snapping your fingers? I can't even find us private parties nowadays, and here it is Christmas time and I have sent ads all over town."

"Something will turn up."

"Nothing will turn up. Tomorrow I'm calling Zack. I'll tell him we'll be there next Saturday same as usual. You were just a mite put out, I'll tell him. He'll understand."

"No, he won't, because I ain't showing. Me and Evie are going to the movies."

"Suit yourself, then," David said. And he was quiet for the rest of the ride, although he whistled under his breath.

When they dropped David off at his house, Drum
jerked his chin toward the front seat. "Come up here
and sit," he said.

"What for?"

"Come talk to me."

She looked at his face in the rear-view mirror. It was
pale and shadowed. And after she had settled herself
beside him he said, "I made a fool out of myself, didn't
I?"

"Oh, no."

"Seems like I am just going through one of those
low periods. Last Christmas we played at three different
parties; this Christmas they forgot all about us."

"Maybe you need more publicity," Evie said.

"I don't see how I can *get* any more. Oh, pretty soon
he will fire me for Saturdays too, I can feel it coming.
I will have to play at those free things he has on Sunday
afternoons, everybody drinking coffee. That's how low
I'll come to."

"You just need a good night's sleep," Evie told him.
"Things will look different in the morning."

"Oh, sure, I know."

When they got home, he pulled off his shirt and jeans
and then climbed into bed with a jelly glass half full of
bourbon. He watched Evie while she moved around the
room straightening up. She folded his clothes and laid
them in a chair, she changed into her seersucker nightgown and then stood before a mirror to curl her hair.
From one of her drawers she took a plastic barrette and
pinned her bangs back. They would have to be trained
that way. She planned to leave her forehead bare again,
showing Drum and all the rest of the world what his
music was worth to her.

"This business about Saturdays," Drum told her. "I
ain't going to change my mind; I meant it. I don't want

to play there at all any more. Why should I go where I'm not appreciated? I would like to find me something new, switch over. Now, are you going to side with David and start beating me down about this?"

"You know I wouldn't," Evie said.

"Well, I was just wondering."

He set the empty jelly glass on the window sill, and by the time Evie had put the lights out he was asleep.

But Evie stayed awake, long after she had gone to bed. She lay on her back, stiff and still, watching how the cold moonlight frosted the rim of the jelly glass. That had been the last of the bourbon. It was a reckless purchase one weekend when they had extra money, and for two months the bottle had sat in the kitchen cupboard growing sticky and fingerprinted, brought down rarely and measured out carefully. Now how long would it be before they bought more? Their money came in dribbles—five dollars here, fifteen there, sometimes a little from her father who said, "This is for a sweater," or for books, or a new hairdo, making it too explicit for Evie to object, although she never spent it on what he suggested. What they had they kept in billfolds; it wasn't enough for a bank. And it was paid out in dribbles, too, so that the dimestore budget book with its headings—"Mortgage," "Insurance," "Transportation"—seemed unrelated to their lives. They spent it on cigarettes or records, or on a can of artichoke hearts which Drum said he wanted to try just once before he died. When they were poorest they ate stale saltines and spaghetti in dented tins, reduced for quick sale. They turned out coat pockets and dug between sofa cushions. And in the end, more money always dribbled in again.

But now their only income would be from the A & P and the filling station. It wasn't much. If she didn't want Drum pumping gas all day she would have to find

a job, and she even knew where: at the public library.
Her father had told her about a position there, intending
it for Drum. (Money was something her father worried
about. Money and balanced diets.) But how would
Drum ever endure a library? He would sit behind a
circulation desk in spurred boots and a black denim
jacket, sinking lower every time he jabbed a rubber
stamp against an ink pad. It would have to be Evie who
did it, afternoons when school was out. She even
thought she might like it. She pictured herself in a blue
smock, calm and competent, going through a set of
crisp motions with catalogue drawers. When she finally
slept she dreamed she walked up to the Unicorn's band
platform with a stack of historical romances, and one
by one she laid them in Drum's lap. "Thank you," said
Drum, strumming his guitar. "It's what I always
wanted."

But in the morning Drum turned out to be against
the idea. He heard it with his eyes on something far
above the bed, his face smooth and blank and patient.
Then at her first pause he said, "No."

"But don't you see?" Evie asked. "It works out so
well. You would never be pressed into doing some job
you hated; you would know you had me to fall back
on."

"I don't like it," said Drum.

"Well, Drum, I never. Are you one of those people
that doesn't like working wives?"

"No. Well, no, of course not. But it wouldn't look
good. People will say I must have got cut back at the
Unicorn."

"You have," Evie wanted to say, but she didn't. She
had read in *Family Circle* about how wives needed tact
at times like this.

On Monday afternoon, she passed the library twice

very slowly and then made up her mind and walked in.
All she wanted to do was satisfy her curiosity. She
smelled the familiar library smells, paste and buckram
and polished wood, and she saw how the cheerful yellow curtains framed narrow rectangles of winter light.
Behind the desk sat Miss Simmons, red-haired and
spectacled, sliding pencils into an orange-juice can
some child had painted for her. "Why, Evie," Miss
Simmons said. "How nice to see you."

"I only came by for a minute," Evie said. She shifted
the heap of books she held against her chest.

"Was there something I could help you with?"

"Oh, no. Well, I was curious, is all; my father said
you had a job open."

"That's right, Naomi's job. She got married. I hated
to lose her. Are you interested?"

"Well, I don't know. There's my, Drum, he doesn't—
but it sounded like something I'd like."

"It's after school hours, you know. No problem
there."

"Yes, I know, but—"

"Dollar and a half an hour."

"Would it take up any evenings?"

"Evenings, no, we're not open evenings. Three to
six every afternoon; you'd be home in time for supper.
Won't you think about it? I'd love to have someone I
knew."

Miss Simmons had a wide, lopsided smile that
changed the shape of her face, making her look young
and hopeful. When she smiled Evie said, "Oh well, all
right. I think I'd like to," without even planning it.
Drum was in some far unlighted corner of her mind.
She wouldn't think about him until later. She followed
Miss Simmons into the workroom behind the desk, still
carrying her books, listening carefully while the job

was explained to her. "Could you start today?" Miss Simmons asked. "There are all these cards piled up. Oh, I hope you like it. Some people get the fidgets in libraries. It's the importance of details that bothers them."

But to Evie, importance of details seemed peaceful and lulling. She settled herself on a high stool in the workroom, with an electric heater warming her cold stockinged feet and a mug of cocoa at her elbow. For three solid hours she alphabetized Library of Congress Cards and stacked them in neat little piles. Abbott, Anson, Arden—the cards snapped crisply under her fingers, and when she had finished with the A's she evened up the corners, slipped a rubber band around them, and moved smoothly into the B's. "Are you getting tired?" Miss Simmons called. "Do you want to take a break? I know this must seem tedious." But Evie didn't get tired all afternoon. At six o'clock, when Miss Simmons moved around the reading room closing blinds and straightening magazines, Evie was sorry to have to go.

Drum was lying on the couch at home with an old copy of *Billboard*. "What took you so long?" he asked.

"I stopped by the library."

"Oh," Drum said.

"Do you—shall I open up some chili?"

"Sure, I reckon."

He never asked what she had been doing at the library.

She went to work every day that week. Although Miss Simmons kept up a steady patter of tea-party talk Evie stayed silent, soaking up the words and the warmth from the heater as she filled out overdue-reminders. Sometimes she wandered through the reading room with a trolley of books to shelve, and the memorized classification numbers hummed peacefully through her head while she searched for shelf-space. Or she sat behind the circulation desk, swiveling in a wheeled metal chair and stamping first books and then cards—thump-tap, thump-tap—until she was lulled into a trance. People rarely spoke to her. If Violet came by and said, "Hi, Evie. Evie?," Evie looked up with a blank smile for several seconds before she realized who it was.

"Oh, aren't you just bored out of your *mind*?" Violet asked. "I don't see how you stand it here."

"It's all right," Evie said.

She kept preparing explanations for Drum—how Miss Simmons was desperate, how the job was only temporary—but she didn't have to use them. Drum asked no questions at all. On Friday he said, "It's my late night at the A & P. Can you come early so I can have the car?"

"I have to stay at the library till six," Evie told him.

"Well, I'll come pick you up and take you home, then. That all right?"

"I guess so."

At six o'clock she looked up from the desk to find him leaning in the doorway, looking sleepy. "I'm ready any time you are," he told her. She had never thought it would be so easy. She wondered if he were just waiting till they were alone to say, "Hey. What's this? I thought I said I didn't want you working." But even after they had left the building, he kept quiet. She had him drop her by the bank to cash her paycheck, and when she returned to the car she handed him the money. "Good, I'm out of cigarettes," he said. She was relieved, but she had a let-down feeling too.

Meanwhile nothing seemed to have been settled with the Unicorn. Friday night David stopped by the house and said, "I wanted Drum, but maybe you could tell me. What am I supposed to do about this Unicorn business? I been letting it ride; I never thought he'd go this far. Now tomorrow is Saturday and we still don't know if Drum will change his mind and play there.''

"He hasn't mentioned it," Evie said.

"Shall I just go on and say we'll show? I thought of it. But then Drum could always make a liar of me, and that's bad for business." He sat down on the edge of the couch. He was still wearing the suit he sold insurance in, gray wool with a pinstripe. It made him look unusually straight-edged and sure of himself. "*You're* around him all week," he said. "And you know he likes the Unicorn. Even I am sure of that much. So what should I do? You must have *some* idea."

"David, I don't. Really."

"But if you don't take the decision out of his hands he might just say no from pride. You know how he is."

"Well," Evie said.

"Shall I do it?"

"He *is* proud."

"So shouldn't I go and tell Zack he's coming?"

"Well, I don't know. I guess you could."

"Good enough," David said. "It'll work out. You'll see."

And it did. On Saturday night she talked Drum into his singing clothes, polished his boots and set them beside the door, followed him around holding his guitar out level, like a tray, until he grew nervous about its safety and yanked it away from her. "Why are you doing this to me?" he asked.

"I'm not doing anything to you, I'm saving you from making a mistake. You'll be sorry later if you throw this job away."

"Don't you care how I feel about it?"

"Of course I do, that's why I'm telling you to go."

"Well, I won't," said Drum. He sat down sharply

and laid his guitar on the couch. Already he was almost
late. Evie kept sliding her eyes toward her watch, on
which time seemed to pass with a hurried, grating motion that she could feel against her skin. "Drum," she
said, "I stuck my neck out for you, I and David both.
I got him to patch things up with Zack. Now what will
Zack say when you don't show up?"

"Well, you had no business doing that," said Drum.

"What else could I do? You always *used* to like the
Unicorn."

"I got a right to change my mind, ain't I?"

"Not when there's nothing to change *to*."

Drum was quiet. She thought that she had lost, and
already her mind was rearranging itself to accept the
defeat when Drum said, "All right. All right."

"You're going?"

"I don't see I have much choice."

At the Unicorn he played heavily, for once overcom-
ing the drums behind him. He did his speaking out
without ceasing to twang the guitar strings, so that his
voice fought out from beneath the notes like a swimmer
beneath the peaks of waves.

"How did it gray?
"When were they pink?
"They've made him a major.
"How long did it take?"

His audience kept silent.

School stopped over the Christmas holidays, but Evie
hardly noticed. She went less and less often now. When
she did go the sharp rhythm of electric bells and the
herding from class to class seemed misted and foreign.
Her teachers spoke in loud, evenly paced voices, em-
phasizing the names of authors and the dates of wars;
students scribbled frantically in looseleaf notebooks,

taking down every word, but what Evie wrote trailed off in mid-sentence. She often stared into space for long periods of time without a thought in her head. When she collected herself, whole minutes might have passed. There was not even an echo of what the teacher had said, and her classmates, still bent over their notebooks, seemed to have ridden away from her on their scurrying ball-point pens. "Please excuse Evie D. Casey," Drum wrote in his notes to the principal. "She was not feeling well and couldn't come to school 'Wednesday,' 'Thursday,' and 'Friday.' Sincerely Bertram O. Casey." Mr. Harrison put on his clear-rimmed glasses and puzzled out the penciled words, bunchy and downward-sloping. The notes were an embarrassment to him. To have her husband write them seemed a mockery, yet her father could not logically be asked to do it instead.

For Christmas, Evie gave her father a pair of gloves and Drum a sweater. Drum gave her a bottle of perfume—"My Sin," which pleased her. She put up a little tree and they had Christmas dinner at the Caseys. Then the next day she went back to work in the library. Miss Simmons had offered her a week's vacation, but Evie felt they couldn't give up the money.

Evenings, when she came home, the house would be filled with the clutter of Drum's day--overflowing ash trays, empty record jackets, stray dishes in the sink. "Were you practicing?" she asked him, but he rarely had been. "I don't know, I just can't get started right," he said. "Seems like I am messing around all the time. My fingers forget what they was doing." He talked more now. His voice tugged constantly on the hem of Evie's mind, so that she almost forgot how it had been in the old days when he never talked at all. "What is the point in me sitting here strumming? I'll never get anywhere.

I ain't but nineteen years old and already leading a slipping-down life, and hard rock is fading so pretty soon nobody won't want it.''

"That's not true," Evie said.

"Well, it *feels* like it is. Feels like I have hit my peak and passed it. I was just a fool to ever hope to be famous."

"Will you *stop* that?" Evie said.

She wanted to get pregnant. She had latched on to the idea out of the blue, flying in the face of all logical objections: her job, their lack of money, the countless times that Drum had whispered, in the dark, "Is it safe?" The thought of a baby sent a shaft of yellow light through her mind, like a door opening. Yet getting pregnant was turning out to be easier said than done. Drum in this new mood of his often drifted into sleep while listening to the radio, a weighted, formless figure face-down on the living room couch. "Drum," she would say, "aren't you coming to bed?" Then he would stagger up and into the bedroom, where he fell asleep again with all his clothes on. She tugged at his boots, working against the dead heaviness of his legs. She put on her nightgown, and in her mirror the bathroom light lit up her silhouette almost as wide as the billowing gown, a blurred stocky figure broadening at the hips and not narrowing below them. She thought of crash diets, exercycles, charm school. When she lay down, Drum would be snoring. She stayed awake for hours with all her muscles tensed, as if she were afraid to trust her weight to the darkness she rested on.

13

In February a revivalist named Brother Hope came to preach at the Pulqua Tabernacle of God. His anxious face appeared in every store window, above interchangeable numerals showing the number of souls he had saved. His sermon titles were posted on a signboard on the Tabernacle lawn: "One-Way Street," "Do You Have a Moment?" and "For Heaven's Sake." Above the signboard were strings of pennants, triangular like the ones in Mr. Casey's filling station.

"Someone is shouting your name in the Tabernacle of God," a bass player told Evie. Evie felt a sort of inner jolt, a bunching together of the chest muscles. Then the bass player said, "You ought to go hear, they say it's right comical."

"Have *you* been?" Evie asked.

"Naw. I don't go places like that."

None of the Unicorn's musicians did; yet still they sieved the news from unnamed sources and passed it on. False gods were multiplying on every corner of the earth, Brother Hope said, even in this green and pleasant town of Pulqua: drugs, liquor, and the mind-snatching rhythms of rock-and-roll. Right here in Pulqua some poor girl had ruined her face during an orgy over a roadhouse rock singer, it was in all the newspapers, and if that was not idolatry then what was?

Evie Decker was her name, if no one believed him; the Unicorn was where the singer sang.

"At least it's publicity," Evie said.

"Publicity won't do us no good in the Tabernacle of God," David told her.

"Well, I don't know why not."

"Do you think that congregation is likely to show up at the Unicorn?"

But he was wrong. They did show up. Not the entire congregation but at least the younger members, probably slipping out on their straight-backed country parents. They came that Saturday in small clusters, pale and watchful, as if Brother Hope had been their trained guide on the paths to sin. The tables were lined with dressed-up boys and dowdy young girls who seemed hit in the face by every beat of the music. Drum slid his pelvis easily beneath the spangled guitar. Evie's scars shone like snail tracks. Brother Hope's congregation leaned forward to watch and then back to whisper, taking in the sights in small gulps. "Well, this is the place all right," Evie heard one boy say. "There's the girl. This is the music." When she rose to meet Drum in back, she walked slowly and proudly, as if she were carrying something important.

That Saturday she was happy. She felt that things were going well again. But by Monday everything had changed. Zack Caraway drove out in person to say that Drum was no longer needed, even for Saturdays. He stood in the middle of the room looking around him unhappily, twisting his hat in his hands. "I was going to say it two nights ago," he said, "but they was a rush toward the end and I put it off. Now, all I've had this winter is bad luck and I know you will argue, Drum, but what can I do? My money has *went*. If you want to come on Sundays to the free-for-all, I would be right happy to have you, but that's the most I . . ."

Drum never said a word. She had expected another fight, but he just sat in the couch with his face toward the window, his long brown eyes reflecting the winter light, not even protesting as Zack cut the last inch from him. After Zack had left he drank two beers and listened to a record. Then David came by, and they played a game of darts. Drum seemed insulated; if Evie mentioned Zack, he looked away from her and all she saw was the smooth olive line of his cheek.

"Zack is slipping," David told her. "If he had eyes he could see that what that Tabernacle crowd is after is you and Drum."

"Well, tell him that."

"*I* can't tell him."

"Somebody should. Brother Hope is giving the Unicorn free publicity and nobody even takes advantage of it."

Publicity was everything. She felt that more and more. She thought of publicity as the small, neat click that set into motion machines that had previously been disengaged. Drum's music, beating like a pulse, had started leaving her ears with a cotton-wool feeling, and his speaking out was harder to understand with every show; but if there were crowds of screaming fans, then everything would click into working order. "If we could only *spread* Brother Hope," she said. "Get his sermons where they mattered more—not just to little old scared country people."

"No way of doing *that*," David said.

"Why not? We could go to the Tabernacle and make a big fuss, get a newspaper write-up."

"Naw," David said.

But she wore him down. Over a two-day period she filled his mind with pictures—Brother Hope looking startled, a reporter asking what all the trouble was about, a news item on Drum Casey's protest at a church attack. David moved forward inch by inch, balking sometimes so that she wished she could just give up. There was too much expected of her, she thought. All this arguing, urging, encouraging. Alone, she heard the driving rhythm of her own voice echoing wordlessly through her mind. But there was Drum. She watched him when he wasn't looking, and felt hollow with worry when she saw him slumped on the couch endlessly circling the rim of a beer can with his index finger. "Oh, why not, let's go and give Brother Hope a try," David said one evening. Drum didn't even look up.

And when David came by Thursday night and said, "You ready?" Drum said, "Ready for what?"

"The Tabernacle of God, of course," David said.

"You wouldn't catch me dead in the Tabernacle of God."

"Well, what the hell, Drum, where you been all this time? We been discussing the Tabernacle three days now and you never said a word against it."

"Oh, never mind," said Evie. "We'll go alone. It's only for a couple of hours."

"Then what about me?" Drum asked.

"You said you didn't want to come."

"Well, what am I supposed to do, just sit here till you get back? Looks like everyone is *leaving* me all the time."

"Lord," said David.

So they all went. They rode in David's Jeep. Wind whistled in under the canvas flaps, and Evie shivered inside her thin school coat and huddled closer to Drum's side. Her hair was pulled straight off her forehead, held by a flaking gold barrette. When she looked into the rear-view mirror her scars glinted back at her, right side to, but dim as an old photograph. Her features were wavery and uncertain. "Now that we're really going I feel like a fool," she said. "I don't even have a plan in mind."

David said, "Well, I did call that photographer from the newspaper. Publicity's no good without a photograph."

"If I hear that word publicity again," Drum said, "I'm going to puke."

"Now, Drum."

The Tabernacle was on Main Street, an old white clapboard house between a pizzeria and a shoe repair shop. A sign cross the porch said, "Pulqua Tabernacle of God. Everybody 'Welcome.' Come on in Folks," with the sermon title tacked beneath it: "What Next?" Nailed to a pillar was another of Brother Hope's posters, with his eyes unfocused and frightened, as if he could see straight to hell. Spinsters in high-heeled galoshes and old men in suit jackets and overalls filed past the poster toward a brightly lit door. Evie followed, holding tightly to Drum's hand so that nothing would separate them. She had pictured something bigger and more anonymous, like a lecture hall; not this oversized front parlor lined with folding chairs and hung with dusty curtains. An old lady with lace laid across her shoulders like antimacassars pressed Evie's hand in both of her own. "Good evening, children, you won't regret this," she said. When she saw Evie's forehead she smiled harder and gazed far away, blinking several times, as if she had received an insult she wanted to overlook. Evie clutched Drum's and David's elbows and led them toward the chairs in the back of the room.

"I wish we hadn't come," she said.

"Told you so," said Drum.

"Well, I forgot how creepy these places are. I don't like the smell."

David was the only one who stayed cheerful. "Smells all right to *me*," he said, and he took a deep breath of

the air—dry wood, hand-me-down hymnals, and dust.
"Yonder is the photographer," he told Evie.

"What's he doing way up front?"

"He has to be far enough away to photograph us."

"Us?" Evie said.

"Who else?"

"Well, yes, of course," Evie said, but she wished
she had thought this thing through before she came.

Brother Hope appeared on a small raised platform up
front. He was red and knotty-faced, like a man swelling
with anger but choking it down. His hair was plastered
sleekly across his skull; and he wore a long black robe
with a striped woolen scarf hanging from his shoulders.
"All rise," he said. His voice was thin and stifled.

Everybody rose. Forty chairs creaked and snapped.

"I was glad when they said unto me, let us go into
the house of the Lord. 'In the Garden.' "

"In the Garden" sounded strange without a piano.
The women sang in high, sliding voices, as if they were
complaining, and the men made muttering sounds beneath the tune. Evie, who disliked hymns, stayed silent.
When all the verses had been sung they sat down again,
and Brother Hope gripped both sides of the pulpit.

"We are gathered here," he said, "as lone survivors on
a sinking ship. Only you and I know that ship is sinking.
Only you and I seek to find the rotting planks. Art thou
weary? Art thou languid? Then thou art smarter than
thy neighbor, for thou hast seen the water rising beneath
the planks. Last month, my friends, I was in Norville. A
man buying a popular magazine was told that the price
had gone up, and I heard him ask, 'What next?' 'What
next?' he said. Well, that started me thinking, my friends.
What next for *us*, in the life beyond, I thought, if things
continue like they're going now? Today there are women
wearing the garb of men, men in stupors from the fumes

of alcohol and the taste of foreign mushrooms, dancers dancing obscenities in public and everywhere, on every corner of the earth, sacrifices made to false gods and earthly idols. What next? What next?"

His voice stitched in and out of Evie's thoughts, rising above them sometimes as a new topic jolted into view and then submerging while she decided whether to go to school tomorrow, planned a menu, wondered what Drum was thinking with his mouth so straight and set. At her left, David shifted his weight but kept his eyes pinned on Brother Hope. The congregation commented on the sermon during each pause. "It's true. It's true." "Amen." "Ain't that so?" Like poor listeners in an ordinary conversation, they seemed likely to jump up at any moment and interrupt to tell experiences of their own. Only none of them did. Instead, Evie began to worry that it would be she herself who interrupted. Pauses between paragraphs grew longer and quieter, swelling until they might burst forth with her own voice saying something terrible. Ordinary ministers picked a single, narrow theme for each sermon; Brother Hope tried to cover the world in an hour. Faced with the leap from one topic to another, from the evils of pre-teen dating to the inevitability of death and from there to the unnaturalness of working mothers, he kept taking a breath and hesitating, as if he worried about the abyss he had to span; and every time it happened Evie drew in her breath too. She was not certain what would burst forth. She gripped the chair in front of her, and the man who sat in it turned to show her the expectant, circular eyes of a baby.

"Our children are no longer safe," said Brother Hope. "Golden nets are cast to reel them into evil and we say, 'It's only music. *We* had music,' we say, but we had the waltz and 'Mairzy Doats.' My friends, I say

unto you, go into your parlors some night and watch
your children dancing. Is that innocence? I can cite
chapter and verse. A young man driving home from a
jukebox joint crashed into a Good Humor truck and
died; marijuana in his glove compartment. His name
was Willie Hammond, if you care to check on that. A
young girl living within your own town limits slashed
her forehead with the name of a rock-and-roll singer;
ruined her life for nothing. If you don't believe me, her
name was Eve Decker; the singer sang at the—"

"Wait," Evie said. "That's *me*."

She stood up, still gripping the chair in front of her,
and looked around at all the upturned faces. Hearing
her name in public, even when she had expected it, gave
her a ripped-open feeling. She couldn't think why David was smiling at her and nodding. "You take that
back," she told Brother Hope.

"We are all friends here," said Brother Hope.

"Well, *I'm* not. You're speaking libel. Slander. I did
not ruin my life, it was not for nothing. How can you
say such a thing?"

Brother Hope was fiddling with the ends of his scarf
and staring at her forehead. "Please, now, please," he
said. "Any burden you have—"

"I don't have *any* burdens!" Evie shouted. "I didn't
ruin my life, I married him!"

A flashbulb snapped in her face, an explosion of light
that faded to a squirmy green circle. It took her a moment to remember about the photographer. She watched
the circle drift over to Brother Hope's face, and then
she let go of the chair.

"Well," she said finally. "The place he was talking
about is the Unicorn, out on the south highway. The
singer is Drum Casey, who is my husband and just got
fired for—"

"Sit down," Drum said.

"—for the last day of the week he was working. Just got his working time cut day by day, raising his hopes and then lowering them again, and if anybody *really* cared about Christian love they would call up the Unicorn and say, 'Where is Drum Casey? Why isn't he there? We want—' "

Drum rose. "I don't have to allow this," he said.

"Why, Drum."

"Shut up," Drum told her. "Sit down."

"Please, my friends. Please," said Brother Hope, and he looked over either shoulder although there was nothing but a blank wall behind him.

"Drum, I am only trying—"

"She's doing great, Drum," David said.

"You shut up too," said Drum. "I have had enough publicity tonight to put me six feet under. And *you*—" he said, turning suddenly on Brother Hope, who opened his mouth and took a breath, "you and your sacrifices to false gods, that's a bunch of bull. It'd been a hell of a lot more sacrifice if she'd been prettier to begin with. Get going, Evie. We're through here."

He took hold of her arm just above the elbow. He pushed her out ahead of him and Evie went, boneless and watery, knocked sick by what he had said. David had her by the other hand. "Now, then," he kept whispering. "Now, wait. . . ."

They rode home in a swelling, suspended silence, as if this were just another pause in Brother Hope's sermon. David kept clearing his throat. Evie expected to cry but could not. Drum sat beside her with his face set straight ahead, his hands on his knees. Once he drew in his breath as if he meant to speak, but he said nothing.

14

That week's newspaper carried a photograph of Evie hunched forward behind a seated man, as if she were pushing him in a wheelchair. Her face looked surprised. "Evangelist Ends Sojourn in Pulqua," the caption read. "Brother Evan Hope left Pulqua yesterday after two weeks at the Tabernacle of God. He described his stay as 'heartwarmingly successful.' Above, a local teen-ager protests his attack on rock music." Evie threw the newspaper aside, not bothering to show Drum. But the next day David drove all the way out to their house to tell them that Drum had been re-hired at the Unicorn. "You can thank Evie for this," he said. "Word of mouth spread what she did all over town. People kept calling Zack and asking where Drum Casey was."

"What do you know," said Drum. He didn't look up from the magazine he was leafing through. "Anything I hate, it's indecision. I wish Zack would just fire me for good and get it over with."

"When are you going to be satisfied? You got your Saturday nights back, didn't you?"

"Sure. I guess so." Then Drum turned another page of his magazine.

What he had said to Evie at the Tabernacle was buried now, not erased but buried beneath the new grave courtesy he showed toward her. He had never apolo-

gized. For several days he treated her very gently, help-
ing her with the dishes and listening with extreme,
watchful stillness whenever she spoke to him. It was
the most he could do, Evie figured. She shoved down
the Tabernacle memory every time it floated up in her
mind; yet evenings, when they sat doing separate things
in the lamplight, she sometimes wanted to leap up and
ask, "What you said, did you mean it? You must have
or you would never have thought it. But did you mean
it for all time, or just for that moment? Are you sorry
you married me? *Why* did you marry me?" None of
the questions were ones Drum would answer. She kept
quiet, and only watched him from across the room until
he looked up and raised his eyebrows. Then the questions began to occur to her less frequently. Whole days
passed without her remembering, and gradually she and
Drum drifted back to the way they had been before.

Drum returned to his Saturdays at the Unicorn without a word, played his songs and came home as soon
as his last set was over. He never went without Evie.
She felt that her hold on her school work was slipping,
and sometimes she suggested that he go alone while she
studied, but Drum said, "Nah, you can study some
other time. You're so smart, one night won't hurt you."
Yet while he played he stared over her head, never directly at her.

"We went two-ing on the one.
"We went circling on the square.
"We went adding on the divide."

Evie listened without changing expression, clutching
her coat around her for warmth.

She thought she might be pregnant. She pictured her
stomach as a thin, swelling shell, like a balloon, and
since something so fragile had to be guarded with a

half-drawn breath, she put off going to the doctor and
she said nothing to Drum. It was too early yet, she told
herself; and then, as she reached the end of the second
month, it was too late. How could she explain keeping
it a secret so long? What held her back was this thin-
skinned feeling. The baby, she thought, was a boy, still
and grave and level-eyed like Drum, and the picture of
those eyes in such a small face made it seem necessary
to protect him in fierce silence every second of the day.
She made a circle of herself, folding more and more
inward. She carried herself like a bowl of water. At
moments when she opened her mouth to say, "Drum?
Guess what," the sense of something spilling or breaking always changed her mind.

In department stores she picked up free magazines
for expectant mothers and studied every word. Babies,
it seemed, nested in vast jungles of equipment, wheeled
and decaled and safety-railed and vinyl-covered. She
had never been exposed to babies before, and she was
not sure how much of the equipment was essential.
Would it take a Jolly Jumper to keep him happy? Was
it true that babies needed to ride their mothers' backs
in canvas carriers in order to feel secure? And if so,
how would she ever buy it all? She put her name in a
drawing for an English pram, and she clipped a newspaper coupon for a free week of germ-proofed diaper
service. Like a mother cat, she wandered through the
house counting up bureau drawers and staring for long
periods of time into corner cupboards. She hung over
the toilet bowl in the mornings, sick and dizzy, and
worried about finding the money for a tip-proof high
chair with a snap-on tray and safety straps.

Meanwhile Drum sat in the bedroom chair with his
feet slung over one of its arms, and for hours on end
he played his guitar. He sang very softly, reaching for

notes deep on the scale. Even Evie could tell the songs
weren't rock. "St. James Infirmary" he sang, and
"Trouble in Mind," and something called "Nobody
Knows You When You're Down and Out." The words
slid about more, the beat was not as clear, and the tunes
were sadder. Evie said, "Did you make these things
up?"

"Shoot, no," said Drum.

"They're not rock, are they?"

"Shoot, no."

It had been weeks since he had written any rock music. At the Unicorn he did the same pieces he always
did, but at home he played nothing but these new ones.
Evie began to recognize them. She could pick out the
patterns, the verses that recurred with only slight vari-
ations from song to song. The parts that she liked she
sang alone in the kitchen, with the tunes all wrong:

One morning you'll wake to an empty bed,
You'll bury your eyes and bow your head.

But she never told Drum she liked them. If he started
playing those things in the Unicorn it would be the end of
him. How could people dance to "Nobody Knows You"?

"You never write any songs these days," she said.

"I'm getting weary of them."

"What will you do, then?"

"Ah, I don't know. Seems like I am always pushing
to lift something I don't have the muscles for. Every
song I wrote, I thought, 'This is it. This is something
singular,' I thought, but later I see how it is no different from anyone else's except maybe worse. Little old
crabbed, stunted lines. Nothing new. Same old beat.
Now, why would I want to write more of them?"

His lashes cut across his eyes, straight and even; his

pupils seemed pricked by tiny points of gold. Evie
touched the hand that lay nearest her on the couch.
"Everything will work out," she said. "This is just a
low period. What you need is publicity."

"Publicity. Huh."

"Let me think about it a while."

"Forget it, I tell you."

"Well, it's for your own good, Drum."

"Not for *my* own good, no ma'am," Drum said. "I
hate it."

"How will you get ahead, then, if nobody knows
your name?"

"That's *my* business."

"It's mine too. It was me you were complaining to."

"I wasn't complaining, I was talking," said Drum.
"And you weren't listening. You were thinking about
publicity, which makes me tired. And I am tired too of
getting nagged at all the time and having to face that
nagging forehead of yours. I don't know why you don't
wear bangs anymore."

"I don't wear bangs because I don't back down on
things I have done," said Evie. "And I have never said
a nagging word to you in my life."

"All right, all right."

"Have I?"

"No, forget it. I was just talking. Evie," he said,
"where has my luck gone? When am I going to rise
above all this? Am I going to grow old just *waiting*?"

But Evie couldn't answer that. All she could do was
sit quiet, leaning gently toward him as if that would do
what words could not, watching him run his fingers
through the slant of his hair.

That Sunday David came over for lunch. While Drum
was in the kitchen opening beers, Evie said, "Listen,

David. What would you think of Drum getting kidnapped?''

"Huh?''

"For publicity.''

"Evie. You couldn't even fool a traffic cop with a
stunt like that.''

"I know we couldn't," Evie said. She looked toward
the kitchen, checking on Drum, and then she came to
sit beside David on the couch. "But listen to what I
have in mind. It wouldn't be a *serious* kidnapping,
nothing to call in the FBI for. He would be spirited
away by fans, that's all, just for a couple of hours. What
would be the harm? And still the newspapers would
pick it up.''

"Sure," said David. "Nothing wrong with that at
all, except it's too much work. It's not worth it.''

"It is to me. *I* will do the work. I'll get Violet and
maybe Fay-Jean Lindsay, she'll do it if she thinks it's
tied up with the Unicorn. And Fay-Jean might have a
friend. I'll arrange the whole thing. All right?''

"You can't arrange Drum," David said.

"Drum?''

"He will never go along with this, you know that.''

"I'm not going to tell him about it.''

"Oh, well, wait now.''

"It's for him, David. I know he doesn't like things
like this, but *I* don't like seeing him just curl up around
the edges, either. What else can I do? Besides, I have
to think about the baby.''

"What baby?''

"I believe I might be having one," said Evie, and
she felt something lurch inside her just the way she had
expected it to.

"Oh," David said. "You are?''

"Don't tell Drum.''

"Well, shouldn't—"

"Evie," Drum called, "what have you done with the beer-can opener?"

"Coming," Evie said. "Listen, David. If I did the work, would you go along with it?"

"Oh, Evie, I don't—"

But at the end of the afternoon, when Drum and Evie were seeing him to the door, David said, "Evie, you know I would always try to help you in any way you wanted."

"Well, thank you," Evie said.

"What was *that* about?" Drum asked when they had shut the door.

"I don't know," Evie said.

In the library she looked up Fay-Jean's number and then reached for the telephone. Even before she had dialed, her throat prepared itself for the tone she wanted. She slipped into it like a needle into a groove: the sure and reasonable voice needed to lay plans before people whom she did not expect to agree with her.

On Tuesday evening at seven, Drum said, "Why are we waiting so long to eat? I'm starved."

"In a minute," Evie said. She stood in the living room window, pressing her face against the glass so that she could see past her own reflection.

"You ain't even started cooking."

"In a minute, I said."

A pair of headlights swung up the road, recognizable even at this distance. The headlights were round and close-set, like the eyes of some small worried lady. They floated gently up and down, bouncing on the uneven road. "Who's that coming?" Drum asked.

"I don't know."

"Who's it *look* like?"

"I don't know."

Drum sighed and moved up next to her. She could smell the marigold smell of his skin. "That's David's Jeep, as any fool can see," he said.

"Is it?"

The Jeep parked in the dirt yard, but the lights stayed on. A minute later there was a knock at the door, and when Drum said, "Come in," the three girls entered first—Violet, Fay-Jean, and Fay-Jean's sister Doris, all dressed up. David came behind. "Well, hey," Drum said. He nodded to Violet and Fay-Jean, and then looked toward Doris and waited to be introduced. No one bothered. The three of them kept walking until they had surrounded him. Then Fay-Jean brought out a shimmering length of nylon cord and reached for one of his hands. For a minute it looked as if it would be as easy as that—just tie him up while he stood waiting. But as her fingers were circling his wrist, Drum said, "What in—" and jerked away. "What the hell's going on?" he said.

"They're kidnapping you," Evie told him.

"They're—"

"Kidnapping. It's only for publicity."

"Are you out of your head?"

"Now wait," David said. "It's not such a bad idea, Drum. We're taking you to my shed. Evie will tell the police a bunch of crazy fans got you, and then you'll be returned. No more than an outing."

"You have went too far this time," Drum said, but it wasn't clear whether he was speaking to David or to Evie. He backed away, holding both arms ready at his sides, while the three girls advanced. "I would help you," David told them, "but it wouldn't look right." Fay-Jean made another pass with the nylon cord and

Drum lashed out, clipping the side of her face with his forearm and sending her crashing into the wall. "Ouch," she said. "Get him, Doris!"

But it was Violet who got him. All she did was fling herself against him like a pillow, knocking him flat on his back. She set her one hundred and eighty pounds squarely on his chest. Even though he was still hitting out at them, Fay-Jean and Doris between them managed to tie his wrists together. Then they all sat there, breathing hard, and Drum lay scowling on the floor. "This is laughable," he said.

"Well, sure," said Violet. "So laugh. Enjoy yourself. We're only going for a little ride."

"*Oh*, no."

He heaved until they couldn't sit on him any longer. He tripped Violet with one kick of his foot and rammed an elbow into Doris's stomach. "Now, you better stop that," Doris said. Her voice was on the edge of tears. "Didn't anybody ever tell you not to go hitting girls?"

"Here," Violet said, and tied his feet together with enough space between them so he could walk. Then they raised him up, keeping tight hold of his elbows.

"Evie," Drum said.

Evie pressed both hands together and shook her head.

"Now, Evie, I know this was your idea. It couldn't be nobody's else's. You tell these girls to let me go, right this second. I don't adapt well to being kidnapped."

"It's only for a while," Evie said.

"I mean it, Evie."

"I packed you a supper. It's in the Jeep. A brown paper bag."

"David?"

David hesitated.

"The worst part's over anyway," Evie told him.

"She's right, Drum. No point untying you now. If I'd of known you'd take it so hard I would have said no, but what have you got to lose? You'll be back by bedtime."

Drum seemed to have nothing more to say. When David had opened the door, the girls led him out with no trouble at all.

After the Jeep had driven off, Evie sat on the couch for a while with her hands pressed together. She had not expected a kidnapping to be so difficult. The room was a shambles—furniture kicked over, cushions and papers scattered across the floor. When she finally crossed to the closet for her coat she nearly tripped over the rug, which lay in a twisted heap. She closed the door behind her before she had even put her coat on and ran toward the Volkswagen.

More headlights floated down the road, wide apart and rectangular. While she stood waiting beside the VW the other car drew to a stop, and a man said, "Evie?"

"Sir?"

"It's me. Mr. Harrison."

"Oh, Mr. Harrison," Evie said. As if this evening had been none of her doing, she felt shaky and relieved at the sight of him. "Drum's been kidnapped," she said. "Not for real, but a bunch of fans got him. What'll I do? I'm getting worried." And she was. Her throat muscles knotted, and that uneven heartbeat was beginning in her ears again.

"Drum can wait," Mr. Harrison said. "Your father's sick. I want you to come with me."

"Drum's been *kidnapped*."

"Evie, we haven't got time for that. Your father's in the hospital."

"Will you *listen*?" Evie said. She had drawn closer to the car now. Her hands clutched the window frame;

she felt them trembling. "Drive me to where Drum is. No, never mind, I'll drive myself. Do I have the keys? Tell my father I'll be there soon. It doesn't matter about the police, just tell my—"

"Your father," said Mr. Harrison, "has had a heart attack and is dying. I didn't want to say it but I see I had to. Climb in. I'll take you to the hospital."

He opened the door on the passenger side, flooding the car with a dingy yellow light. Evie circled the car and climbed in slowly.

"Hospital," she said. Her voice was as clear and sudden as if it were an order, but she was merely echoing him without any idea at all of what to do next.

※

15

In the hospital lobby, on a sectional vinyl couch, sat Mrs. Harrison and Mrs. Willoughby, the old lady who lived next door to Evie's father. They stood up when Evie entered—a bad sign. Evie and Mr. Harrison clicked toward them across polished tiles, between potted palms and standing ash trays. As they came up to the two women, Mrs. Harrison tugged her skirt down and straightened her belt and smoothed the gray pom-pom of hair on her forehead. "Evie, dear—" she said. Her tone made everything clear, there was no need to say more, but Evie was in the grip of a stony stubbornness and she refused to understand. "How is he?" she asked.

"He passed, dear," Mrs. Willoughby said. Mrs. Willoughby was as small and as dumpy as a cupcake, raising her creased hands to her bosom and furrowing her powdery face into sympathy lines. Everyone else was small too. The scene was miniaturized and crystal-clear, like something seen through very strong prescription glasses. Lights were sharp pinpoints. Sounds were tinny.

"Would you like to see him?" Mrs. Harrison asked.

"No, thank you," said Evie.

"It happened not long after you left, Bill. I wished

you had known, so as to prepare Evie. I thought of coming out after you.''

''Well,'' said Mr. Harrison. ''This is very very sad news. Very sad. Sam Decker was as fine a man as I've known. How long have we known him, Martha?''

''Oh, years. Since back before—Evie, we will expect you to come stay the night. You don't want to go all the way out to your place again, do you?''

''I think I'll go to my father's,'' Evie said.

''Oh, no, dear. Not alone.''

''I'd rather.''

''Well, anything you say. If it were *me*, though—''

They drove there in Mr. Harrison's car. Mrs. Willoughby sat in back, and Evie was urged to wedge herself in the front seat between the Harrisons. Touches kept grating against her—Mr. Harrison's elbow as he shifted gears, Mrs. Harrison's sharp-edged purse, her cold gloved fingers patting Evie's wrist. Every now and then Mrs. Harrison clicked her tongue and shook her head. ''Such a patient man, he was,'' she said. ''Oh, and all those troubles. First his wife passing—well.''

''He was just leaning across the fence, like,'' Mrs. Willoughby said. ''He said, 'Mrs. Willoughby, all my potted plants are dying. I don't understand it.' 'It's that maid of yours,' I told him. 'Not that I have any proof, but in my heart I feel she neglects them. Yellowy leaves never pinched off, a sort of unwatered look to the soil. I could be wrong,' I said. Or meant to say, but then he took in a breath and opened his mouth and slumped over. I couldn't get straight what had happened. I said, 'Mr. Decker? Why, Mr. Decker!' The fence held him up. He seemed to be resting.''

''Now, now,'' said Mrs. Harrison.

'' 'All my potted plants are dying,' he told me. Oh, little did he know!''

"Now, now."

They stopped in front of Evie's father's house, where all the lights still blazed. At first they planned to come in and keep her company, but Evie wouldn't allow it. "I'd rather be alone," she said.

"Oh, no, dear, not at a time like this. I know it *seems* you'd rather. But we'll be quiet as mice. I'll just make tea and not say a word—"

"No. I mean it."

"Well, maybe Mrs. Willoughby, then."

"Oh, I'd *love* to!" Mrs. Willoughby said.

"No. Thank you."

"Whatever you say, of course," said Mrs. Harrison. "I would think, myself—but that's not important. Just try and get some rest, and we'll be by to talk about the arrangements in the morning."

"Arrangements?" Evie said. She thought of song arrangements, then furniture, then flowers in vases. Meanwhile Mrs. Harrison and Mrs. Willoughby looked at each other in silence, as if there were no possible synonym they could think of to offer her. "Oh. Arrangements," Evie said finally.

"Will you call us if you need anything?"

"Yes. And thank you for all you've done."

"He was a mighty fine man," Mr. Harrison said suddenly. He coughed and looked down at the steering wheel.

Evie and Mrs. Willoughby climbed out of the car and watched it drive off. Against the lighted house Mrs. Willoughby was only a silhouette, topped by a scribble of hair. Charms jingled when she moved. "There is the fence," she said. "He was leaning over it, like. I was standing in that patch of earth, wishing it was spring and time to plant petunias. He came up slow. Leaned his elbows on that fence and said . . ."

She padded away, maybe still talking. Evie waited until she was lost in the darkness before she climbed her own porch steps.

The house had not yet heard of the death. Clocks ticked, the refrigerator whirred, a desk lamp lit an ash tray with a pipe resting on it and the short-wave radio was speaking Spanish. Evie clicked the radio off and then moved through the house, still in her coat. She didn't touch anything. She looked at the dishes in the kitchen sink, then at the bed upstairs which Clotelia had left unmade. She leaned forward to study an oval photograph above the bureau: a woman in a high-necked dress, perfect creamy features curled over the back of a chair, a tail of hair tied low on her neck with a wide black bow. An ancestor, maybe; no one could tell her any more. Under her father's bed two socks lay like curled mice, startling her.

Her old room held a bulletin board, a pennant-covered wastebasket, and the upstairs telephone. Everything else had been borne away by Drum in the U-Haul-It truck. Evie sat down on the floor and pulled the telephone by its tail until it rested between her feet. Then she dialed Clotelia's number.

"Clotelia?" she said.

"Who's this?"

"It's Evie."

"Oh. Hey."

"I'm calling with bad news, Clotelia. My father died."

There was silence. Then Clotelia said, "Oh, my Lord have mercy."

"It was a heart attack."

"Well, Lord have mercy. That poor man. Was he all alone when he passed?"

"He was talking to Mrs. Willoughby."

"Her. I could think of better to die with."

"Well, I was wondering. Could you come stay the night with me? I'll be here till tomorrow."

"Sure thing," said Clotelia. "I be right over. Well, Lord. Did you ever?"

"I'll see you then," Evie said.

She hung up and dialed again. "David?" she said.

"This is his brother. David ain't here."

"Well, this is Evie Decker. Could I speak to Drum Casey? He's out in your shed."

"Shed? What shed is that?"

"Your tool shed."

"Is that a joke or something?"

"He's out in your tool shed."

"What would he be doing out there?"

"Oh, Lord, I don't know," Evie said. "Just messing around. Give him a message then, I don't care."

"Well, I will if I ever run into him."

"Say my father died. Say I'm sorry but I can't bother sending the police after him right now and I'll see him in the morning."

"What?"

"Just tell him to come on home, will you?"

"Oh, well, if I—"

She hung up and started wandering through the rooms again. Now the house was quieting down. Beneath the surface noise of clocks and motors there was a deep, growing silence that layered in from the walls, making her feel clumsy and out of place. Her shoes clacked against the floor boards. Her full coat snatched at ash trays and figurines as she passed them. In the living room her mother smiled hopefully from a filigree frame, her hair tightly crimped and her lipstick too dark, remembered now by no living person. Her father's textbook lay in an armchair on top of a sheaf of graded quizzes. And everywhere she looked there were props to pass time with: completed crossword puzzles, a face made out of used matches, a *Reader's Digest* vocabulary test neatly filled out in pencil.

Clotelia arrived wearing a long striped rope, like one of the three wise men. Her head was wrapped in a silk turban. Darts of gold dangled from her ears. "My Lord, I can't take it in," she said. "The news don't stick in my head. Well, been one of those days, I might have known. Where is your bangs, may I ask?"

"I'm pinning them back now," Evie said.

"You look like trash. Go comb them down. If you want I fix you some cocoa and then you tell me how it come about."

"There's nothing to tell. I wasn't there," Evie said.

But Clotelia only waved a hand and swept on into the kitchen—swept literally, gathering with the hem of her robe all the dust balls she had left behind that day. "Now then," she said as she took down the cocoa box. "Did he pass peaceful? What was his last words?"

"I wasn't there, I said. He wondered why his potted plants were dying."

"Oh, that poor man. Blamed me, I bet."

"He didn't say."

"You don't look good, Evie. How far along are you?"

"What?"

"How far? Two months? Three?"

"Three, almost."

"Oh, my, and never told your daddy. What is it makes you act like that?" She lit the flame under a saucepan of milk. "Well, they is a silver-backed mirror in the guest room he always said he would will to me. He tell you that?"

"No, but you can have it anyway. I don't care," Evie said.

"He give you the house, I reckon. Well, I will say this: He always was a gentleman. Never cause me trouble, like others I could name. Now I got to find me another job."

"You could get yourself a factory job," Evie said.

"Oh, you be roping me in to take care of that baby of yours, I expect."

"Are you crazy? You might sacrifice him up at a Black Panther rally."

"Listen to that. A death night and you talk as mean-mouthed as you ever did. Here, drink your cocoa."

She passed Evie a flowered mug and then leaned back against the sink, folding her arms in her long flowing sleeves. Her hands, striped a soft glowing yellow at the outsides of her palms, gripped her elbows. "And now I hear you quit school," she said.

"Who said that? I never quit."

"Been weeks since you been, I hear."

"Well," said Evie. She ran her finger around the rim of her mug. It was true; she couldn't remember the last time she had attended a class. "Anyway, I'm starting back next week," she said.

"You separated, too, ain't you," said Clotelia.

"Separated?"

"From that husband of yours."

"*No*, I'm not separated."

"Where's he at, then?"

"Oh, at home, I guess."

"Why ain't he here, in your time of trouble? Or why ain't you there?"

"It's complicated," Evie said.

"Oh, I just bet it is. No point in a husband if you ain't going to lean on him during stress, now, is there?"

"Clotelia, for heaven's sake," Evie said. "Will you stop just *harping* at me? Will you leave me *be*?"

"Well. Sorry," said Clotelia. She unfolded her arms and gazed down at her fingernails, shell-pink with half-moons left unpainted. "If I'd of thought, I'd of brought my mother," she said.

Evie put her head in her hands.

"My mother is a consoler at the Baptist Church. She go to all the funerals and console the mourners till they is cheered up."

"How would she go about that?" Evie asked in a muffled voice.

"Oh, just hug them and pat their shoulders, offer them Kleenex. How else would she do?"

Then Clotelia, who was not like her mother at all, turned her back and rinsed out the cocoa pan, and Evie cupped her hands around her mug for warmth.

16

"It's been weeks since I've been out in the country," said Mrs. Harrison. "Wouldn't you think winter would be *over* by now? Look at that sky. Look at those trees, not a sign of green. If you like, I can turn on the heater, Evie."

"I am a little cold," Evie said.

Mrs. Harrison reached for a lever somewhere beneath the dashboard. She drove with a look of suspense on her face, as if she constantly wondered how she was doing. Her back was very straight; six inches separated her from the back of the car seat.

Mr. Harrison couldn't come, of course. It was a school day. Evie understood that but Mrs. Harrison seemed afraid she hadn't. She said, "Oh, if only Bill could have made it. He wanted to, you know that. And naturally he will be coming to the funeral. He feels just terrible about all this. Your father was the first teacher we met when Bill came here to be principal. 'I'm Sam Decker,' he said—Oh, I remember it just as *clear*! Had on that baggy suit of his. There was some confusion in his mind about whether or not I meant to shake hands. And now look. But if Bill was to turn his back for a second, even, that school would just shatter into pieces. 'Bill,' I said, 'Evie will understand. You are coming to the funeral, aren't you?' and he said, 'Martha, you know I am.' I felt sure you wouldn't be insulted.''

"No, of course not," Evie said. "He did more than enough last night."

"Oh, that was nothing," said Mrs. Harrison.

"Well, I did appreciate it."

They seemed to have reached the end of a dance set, both of them curtsying and murmuring a pattern of words. But Evie had trouble remembering what to say. Her voice wandered, searching for the proper tone. Had she shown the right amount of gratitude? Was anything else expected of her? A row of grownups lined the back of her mind, shaking their heads at the clumsiness of Evie Decker.

"You'll have to tell me where to turn, dear. I've never been out this far before."

"Oh. Right up there at the tobacco barn," Evie said.

"Don't you have trouble with undesirable neighbors around here?"

"I don't know any of them."

Mrs. Harrison swung to the right, onto deep clay ruts hardened by frost. It sounded as if the bottom of the car were dropping out. Her gloved hands were tight on the wheel, strained shiny across the knuckles, and she looked anxiously around her while the car seemed to bound on its own accord through the dry fields. Around a curve there were two thin children, ropy-haired, lost in clothes too big for them, holding a dead rabbit by the heels and offering it forth. "My stars," said Mrs. Harrison. She sailed on past them while a narrow line suddenly pinched her eyebrows tighter.

"One thing I told Bill," she said. "I told him, 'Thank heaven she's married, Bill.' We hadn't thought it at the time, of course, but *now* look. You won't be all alone in the world. You have yourself a hand-picked guardian. Are you certain this is the road?''

"Yes. Our house is just over there.''

"Where?''

"There,," said Evie, and she nodded at the tarpaper shack. Yet for a minute, she hadn't been sure herself. It looked different. The sky today was a stark gray-white, arching over treeless billows of parched land and dwarfing the house and the single bush that grew by the door. Blank squares of gray were reflected off the windowpanes. A dribble of smoke rose from the rusted chimney pipe. Mrs. Harrison drove into the dirt yard and parked between a wheel-less bicycle and a claw-footed bathtub, but before she had turned the motor off Evie said, "Oh, don't come in. Really. I'll be all right.''

"Well, are you sure?'' Mrs. Harrison asked.

"I'm positive. Thank you very much.''

"Well. We'll see you at the funeral, then. Or before, if you think of anything you need. You let us know.''

She waited while Evie collected her coat around her and fumbled for the door handle. Then she raised one gloved hand and shot off into the road, still stiff-backed. A spurt of dust hovered behind her.

Evie climbed the two wooden steps, avoiding the corner that was rotting off its nails. When she opened the door she was met by a damp smell, as if the wintry sky had seeped in through the cracks around the windows. It took her a minute to understand why things were in such a jumble; the kidnapping had slipped her mind. A chair lay on its side, poking splintery legs into her path. The shaggy rug, worn down to bare fabric in spots, was twisted beneath it. At the other end of the room there was a half-finished game of idiot's delight on a footstool, a heap of paper airplanes made by Drum on

an idle day, five empty beer cans and an ash tray full of
cigarette butts and chewing-gum wrappers and the metal
tabs from the beer cans. A grape-juice stain on the wall
had seeped through the white poster paint she had covered it with. The room might have been left weeks ago,
hardening beneath its stale film of dust.

"Drum?" she called.

She heard something from the bedroom, not quite a
sound.

"Is that you, Drum?"

By the time she reached the bedroom door, Drum
was already sitting up. One side of his face was creased
from the pillow. Beyond him was Fay-Jean Lindsay,
wearing an orange lace slip which seemed to have
drained all the color from the rest of her. Her face and
her pointy shoulders were dead white; her tow hair
streamed down her back as pale as ice. "*Oh*-oh," she
said, and reached for the black dress crumpled at the
end of the bed. Drum only looked stunned. He and
Evie stared at each other without expression, neither
one seeming to breathe.

"What are *you* doing here?" he asked her finally.

"This is where I live."

"Well, where you been? You think you can just stay
away all night and then pop back in again?"

"I've been home. My father died."

"Oh. Oh, Lord." He looked for help to Fay-Jean,
but Fay-Jean sat among the blankets groping her way
upward through her black dress. Nothing showed but
two limp arms raised toward the ceiling. When her face
had poked through she said, "Well, excuse me for being here but you were away, after all. Will you zip me
up?"

"Certainly," Evie said. Now, too late, she hit upon
the polite tone of voice she had needed for the grown-

ups. She zipped the dress while Fay-Jean held her hair
off her neck; she waited patiently while Fay-Jean trailed
long toes beneath the bed feeling for her spike-heeled
shoes. Meanwhile Drum had risen and was shaking out
his dungarees. He wore yellowed underpants and an
undershirt with a hole in the chest, its neckband frayed.
He hopped one-footed into the dungarees, clenching his
muscles against the cold. "Look," he kept saying.
"Wait. Listen." But nothing more. Evie handed Fay-
Jean her coat and saw her to the door. "How do I get
out of here?" Fay-Jean asked.

"Walk to the highway and catch a bus."

"Walk? In these shoes? Couldn't you just drive me?"

"I don't have the time," Evie said, and shut the door.

She went to the kitchen and began making coffee,
still in her coat. The coat gave her a brisk, competent
feeling. While she was waiting for butter to melt in the
frying pan Drum came out, dressed in his dungarees
and a khaki shirt, and stood behind her. "Well, I don't
know what to say," he said.

Evie tilted the frying pan, evening the butter.

"And then about your father. Well. He was a right
nice guy."

She rapped an egg and broke it, neatly.

"I don't know what got into me," Drum said. "It
was that kidnapping. How could you do me that way?
And then it looked like you had decided not to come
back again. Either that or forgot all about it. We waited
and waited, those three girls just tapping around the
tool shed. Violet trying to start up campfire songs. Evie,
say something. What are you thinking?"

"I am thinking that we have to get organized," Evie
said. "Have you ever *looked* at this place? It's a mess.
And I'm freezing to death, it's much too cold."

"Well, is *that* what you want to talk about? *House-keeping?*"

"Not housekeeping, just things in general. You've got to pull yourself together, Drum. I keep meaning to tell you this: I'm expecting a baby. It's coming in six months or so."

She scrambled the eggs around rapidly, not looking at him. Drum said nothing. Finally she let out her breath and said, "Did you hear me?"

"I heard."

"Well, you don't act like it."

"It just took me by surprise, like," Drum said. "Why didn't you mention this before?"

"I was waiting for the right time."

"Is *this* the right time?"

Then she did look at him, but she couldn't tell what he was thinking. He leaned against the wall with his boots crossed, his eyes fixed on the swirling eggs, so that all she could see were the straight dark lines of his lashes. "Right time or not," she said after a minute, "we are going to have to make some arrangements. Now, my father has left me his house. We can move in this afternoon—just pack up and leave this place. Start a new life. Give some shape to things."

"You mean *live* there? Live in his house?"

"It's our house now."

"It's *your* house."

"Well, what's the difference?"

"I like it where we are," Drum said.

"We can't stay here, Drum."

"I don't know why not."

"We just can't."

"Well, I can't go *there*," said Drum.

"What do you mean?"

"What I said. I can't do it."

He sat down at the kitchen table, bracing himself with his hands as if he had a headache. Evie stared at him, but he wouldn't say any more. He folded his arms on the table and waited. She poured his coffee, dished out his eggs, and found him a fork. Then she said, "All right. I'll go there alone."

"You mean leave me?"

"If I have to."

"You don't have to," said Drum. "Evie, I don't know why you are talking this way. Is it Fay-Jean? Fay-*Jean* don't mean nothing. I swear it. Oh, how am I going to convince you?"

"Fay-Jean. Don't make me laugh," said Evie. "All I'm asking is for you to pick yourself up and move to a decent house with me. If you don't do it, then it's *you* leaving *me*. I did give you the choice."

"That's no choice," Drum said. "Evie, I would do almost anything for you but not this. Not get organized and follow after you this way. You used to like it here. Can't you just stay and wait till my luck is changed?"

He laid one hand on her arm. His wrist was marked with a chafed red line. Evie felt something pulled out of her that he had drawn, like a hard deep string, but she squared her corners as if she were a stack of library cards.

"I have the baby now," she said.

"I don't see how that changes anything."

"No, I know you don't. That's why I'm leaving."

"Can't we talk about this?"

But he had to say that to her back. She was already leaving the room. She went to the bedroom and pulled out a suitcase, which she opened on the bed. Then she began folding the blouses that hung in her closet. Hundreds of times, in movies and on television, she had watched this scene being rehearsed for her. Wives had laid blouses neatly in overnight bags and had given them a brisk little pat, then crossed on clicking heels to collect an armload of dresses still on their hangers. There was no way she could make a mistake. Her motions were prescribed for her, right down to the tucking of rolled stockings into empty corners and the thoughtful look she gave the empty closet.

Drum came to be her audience, leaning awkwardly in the doorway with his hands in his pockets. "You are moving in too much of a rush," he told her.

"What?" said Evie, and she stared down at her hands, overflowing with scarves and headbands.

"People don't just take off like this. They think things through. They talk a lot. Like: How will you support that baby, all alone?"

"I'll get along."

"Yes, well," Drum said. "*That's* for sure." He picked up a barrette from the floor and studied it, turning it over and over in his hands. Then he said, "How will you explain to strangers, having 'Casey' wrote across your face?"

"I'll tell them it's my name," Evie said. Then she paused, in the middle of rolling up a belt. "It *is* my name."

Drum frowned at the barrette. "Now that you have done all that cutting," he said, "and endured through bleeding and police cars and stitches, are you going to say it was just for purposes of *identification*?"

He tossed the barrette into the open suitcase. Evie dragged an airline bag from under the bed, and filled it with underwear and stray bottles from the medicine cabinet. In the bathroom, holding a tube of toothpaste and watching her smudged face in the mirror, she said, "*I* didn't do it."

"What?"

"I didn't cut my forehead. Someone else did."

"You don't make sense," Drum told her.

"Well, you were there. You remember how it was. The singing was good and there were fans shouting back at you and lots of people dancing. When I went into the restroom an argument started up. I forget just how. Me and a redhead and some friend of hers. She got mad. She told her friend to hold me down and she slashed your name on my face. 'I hope you're satisfied,' she said. *That* was how it happened."

"Life is getting too cluttered," Drum said.

"Didn't I tell you so?"

She zipped the airline bag. There were other things of hers all over the house, books and records and pieces of clothing, but all she wanted now was to finish up. In movies the packing did not go on so interminably. She picked up the suitcase, but Drum moved forward to take it away from her. "Evie, don't go," he said.

That was said in movies too. Then the whole scene would end with his changing his mind, saying he would come with her anywhere, but what did Drum know about things like that? "Come with me, then," she said, and all Drum said was, "No. I can't."

He had never once done what she had expected of him.

He carried the suitcase, she carried the airline bag. They crossed the cold dirt yard to the car. "Keys," said Drum, and when she handed them to him he opened the trunk and slid the bags in. He was going to let her go, then. She climbed into the driver's seat and waited for him to slam the trunk lid down. "Maybe—" he said, when he had come around to her side of the car.

She rolled the window down. "What?"

"I said, maybe later you will change your mind. Do you reckon?"

"I never back down on things," Evie said.

He reached in with the keys. He didn't even say good-bye; just laid the keys in the palm of her hand, leaving her with a trace of his cool, slick surface and a smell of marigolds and a brief tearing sensation that lasted long after she had rolled out of the yard toward town.

On Saturday night at the Unicorn, Joseph Ballew and Drumstrings Casey played rock music on a wooden dance platform, the same as always. Joseph Ballew sang two new songs and Drumstrings Casey sang old ones, stopping his strumming occasionally to speak out between verses.

"Where is the circular stairs?" he asked.

And then, *"But the letters was cut backwards.*

"Would you explain?"

His audience just nodded, accepting what he said. The only person who could have answered him was not present.

ABOUT THE AUTHOR

ANNE TYLER was born in Minneapolis, Minnesota, in 1941 but grew up in Raleigh, North Carolina. She graduated at nineteen from Duke University, and went on to do graduate work in Russian studies at Columbia University. Anne Tyler has written thirteen novels; her eleventh novel, *Breathing Lessons*, was awarded the Pulitzer Prize in 1988. She is a member of the American Academy and Institute of Arts and Letters. She and her husband, Taghi Modarressi, live in Baltimore, Maryland.